DEATH IN OSLO

This is a work of fiction. Names, characters, places, and incidents either are the product of the author's imagination or are used fictitiously, and any resemblance to any persons, living or dead, business establishments, events, or locales is entirely coincidental.

This paperback edition 2024

1

First published in Great Britain by Wallbank Books 2024

The right of Andy Conway to be identified as the authors of this work has been asserted by him in accordance with the Copyright, Designs and patent Act, 1988 © Andy Conway 2024.

ISBN: 9798333608741

All rights reserved. No part of this publication may be reproduced, stored in a retrieval system, or transmitted in any form or by any means, electronic, mechanical, photocopying, recording or otherwise without the prior written permission of the publishers. This book may not be lent, hired out, resold or otherwise disposed of by any way of trade in any form of binding or cover other than that in which it is published, without the prior consent of the publishers.

Cover design by Simon Moody at Wallbank Art.

To

John Powell

The fuel to the fire

1

AT FIRST IT WAS black and silent, as if they were not moving, as if they were trapped in a yawning cavern of Norwegian night. But then they were speeding on a cable-stayed bridge, the headlights of cars rushing in the opposite direction. A chasm of water under them, and for a moment it seemed they were under it, beneath the rushing ice-cold fjord. The air was cold and thin and all Blackwood could think as he was rushing through it was what this monstrous bridge must have cost: the oil and concrete, the steel and the human reputation, the vast sums of money poured into its construction.

And then he was there, in the middle of the bridge, looking down at the water below.

His daughter stood on the edge of the bridge, ready to jump.

Blackwood's heart dropped.

He ran towards her.

The bridge seemed to stretch forever.

He couldn't reach her.

She jumped, and Blackwood woke up with a jolt.

The truck had come to a stop again. He blinked and nodded to Dag, who did not return his smile. For twenty hours, on the long, slow drive from Tromsø, all the way down the strip of land that was Norway, Dag had smiled but said little.

Blackwood peered out at the dim sodium light of an industrial estate.

"Is this Oslo?"

Dag shook his head. "Almost. This is Stovner. One stop before Oslo."

Dag jumped out of the cab and walked off to a line of industrial units.

Blackwood pulled up his phone and hit the Maps icon. A blue dot zoomed in on their location. They were 13 kilometres from Oslo central, only 20 minutes away. It didn't make sense that they would stop for another rest this close to their destination.

He sighed and stretched.

Maybe this was Dag's delivery drop off and the end of the road. Maybe this was where Blackwood would have to get off and make his own way into Oslo. Or maybe Dag would be charitable and drive the twenty minutes and drop him off in the centre. He was at the man's mercy.

Blackwood peered out through the murky orange glow over this industrial estate. There was no sound apart from the distant hum of traffic and the pitter-patter of raindrops on the truck.

He could make out Dag approaching a group of dark figures in the distance. Something about them, the dark clothes, the casual sports gear they all wore, something about the way they lurked, made the hair tingle on Blackwood's neck. A sixth sense he had for danger. A sense he'd had since Desert Storm.

It had seen him through situations that had left other men in a box.

He eased open the truck door and was about to step out when a sharp crack of gunfire pierced the air.

Blackwood instinctively dropped down into the footwell of the truck's cabin, his heart racing with adrenaline. He had heard automatic weapons fire many times before, and it always took him back to Iraq.

He took in a deep breath and tried to reconfigure, the taste of cold, metallic fear in the back of his throat.

He raised his head above the dashboard and checked the side mirror.

A body was prone on the floor. Dag was lying dead.

One of the men was holding his head in his hands.

The other, wielding the gun, slapped him across the face.

He heard the man yelling something but he couldn't make it out.

He held his breath for an eternity, trapped, before the men headed for the truck.

They hadn't seen him, he was sure. Maybe they didn't even know he was travelling with Dag. Blackwood cursed. He should have jumped out of the cab and run for cover. He had to think fast. If they found him, he'd be as dead as Dag.

Their footsteps clunked across concrete.

He had to find a way out. He reached up and opened the roof hatch, squeezing himself out of the small opening.

Lying on top of the truck's cabin, he pressed himself flat against the cold metal surface.

They converged on the truck.

Blackwood held his breath and listened.

The truck shifted as one of them climbed into the cab right under him.

The others went round to the rear of the truck. They hadn't seen him. They didn't know he was there.

A stream of Norwegian. Indecipherable but for a few odd words he recognized: *nei* and *narkotika* and something about a green locker.

Whoever was in the cab, jumped out and joined the others at the rear. The truck shuddered as the doors slid open at the back.

Blackwood used the noise as cover to climb down to the ground, landed as silently as he could, and scooted under the truck to lie in the black shade.

The figures searched the truck and lifted something out. He followed their feet as they carried whatever it was to a nearby car and threw it in the boot.

This was the moment. His chance to escape.

He rolled out from under the truck, out into the open, jumped to his feet and came eye-to-eye with a startled face.

2

IT WAS A BOY. A teenage boy, not the hardened face of a career criminal he'd expected. For a moment, they stared at each other, so close they could almost kiss.

The boy took a breath, ready to scream.

Blackwood headbutted him with a sickening crack.

The boy dropped to the floor with a sharp yelp of pain.

Blackwood grabbed the gun from the boy's hand, swiftly assessing the situation. There were three others, over by the car. He took a deep breath and steadied himself, his heart pounding.

The other three had heard the yell and turned.

Blackwood squeezed off two shots in quick succession.

The men dropped to their knees.

He ran to the cover of a line of bushes, broke through the undergrowth and veered sharp left, rolling to the ground, training the gun on them in a sniper's position.

The men scattered and shouted in Norwegian.

Blackwood tracked them through the screen of the undergrowth. The man he'd headbutted got to his feet, moaning and crying and staggered away.

They shouted among themselves and seemed to be debating if they should hunt him down.

One of them screamed what sounded like *"Kom en!"* and they stumbled back to the car, threw themselves in and started the engine with a roar.

Blackwood exhaled, jumped to his feet and emerged into the light.

Sirens in the distance. That was why they'd run.

Dag's body lay in the same spot they had left him. He was dead. That was clear.

He should have done something sooner. Now it was too late.

Blue lights pierced the black sky. Blackwood tossed the gun into the bushes, ran to the truck and snatched his bag from inside the cab.

He jumped down to the concrete and set off to run back into the undergrowth that edged the industrial estate. Stumbling through the dark wood, he came to a wall and vaulted it to find himself in an alleyway and leapt over a pile of garbage and broken furniture. His heart raced as the sirens grew louder and closer.

He was sure they would find him any second now but he kept running. He ducked out of the alley and found himself in a wide-open stretch of industrial estate again, hopelessly exposed. He clung close to the buildings, hoping to sneak away.

The sirens and blue flashing lights converged and, in an instant, the place was lit up like a nightclub.

A half dozen voices screamed at him to "Halt!"

He turned, resigned to his fate.

The police surrounded him with guns drawn, barking in Norwegian.

He understood, sure enough. He dropped his bag and raised his hands in surrender.

3

The darkened streets of Oslo flashed by as the car roared through the night. Martin sat in the back, trying to ignore the thumping music, the smell of sweet marijuana, and the banter between the driver, Kjetil Bergman, and the two thugs.

Martin glanced at Kjetil as he lit a joint and inhaled deeply. With his leather jacket and shaved head, he seemed unruffled by the chaos they had caused at the industrial estate. He caught Martin looking at him and barked out a short laugh.

"I thought I told you to keep an eye out," he said, blowing a plume of smoke in Martin's direction. He grinned, but there was no humour in his eyes.

Martin resisted the urge to wipe his face with his sleeve. His nose was still throbbing from the stranger's headbutt, and he could feel a trickle of blood drying on his lips. He glanced away, not wanting to show any weakness.

Kjetil laughed again. "It takes a special kind of idiot to run into a brick wall," he said.

The others laughed.

Martin trembled, his body spasming as he remembered the sound of the gunshot. They'd murdered the driver. No one had said anything about murdering the driver. It was supposed to be a simple task; just meet up with the truck and pick up the contraband hidden inside. But with one pull of the trigger, everything had changed. A simple pick-up job. And then everything had gone to hell.

Kjetil glanced in the rearview mirror and spotted Martin's frightened expression. He chuckled. "Hey kid, don't worry. You did good. You were brave."

Martin tapped his foot and rubbed his sweaty palms to distract from the awful stomach cramps. He glanced around, trying to avoid eye contact with the members of the gang. He gripped the door handle to his side, to push it open and dive out.

Kjetil seemed to sense his discomfort and turned to him with a smirk, passing the fat joint. "You'll get used to it," he said. "It's all part of the job. You're part of a team now. You belong here."

Martin tried to ignore the chill that ran through his body as Kjetil turned back to the road. He had always wanted to fit in, but not like this. He took a drag on the joint and felt it soothe his pounding face.

The car drove for a few more minutes until the towering apartment blocks of Grünerløkka came into view. The streetlights were brighter here, and the streets busy with drunks, clubbers, prostitutes. A screaming chaos. Martin let out a long sigh of relief. He was back in the warm embrace of the city.

"Who the fuck was that guy, anyway?" Juli moaned. "That Dag fucker was supposed to be alone."

"Yeah, definitely," Mads complained. "We weren't expecting anyone else. Damn!"

Kjetil shrugged. "Who knows. Some random dude looking for a ride? We'll never know."

Martin swallowed and spoke his fear. "Will he go to the police? He saw my face."

"If I thought he would, I would have to kill him," Kjetil said with certainty. "But he ran. He ran out of there before we'd even left. If he knows what's good for him, he'll keep on running."

They all laughed.

Martin wasn't so sure. He remembered the swift, brutal efficiency of how the man had operated. He was no loser who would crumble at the sight of a small-time criminal like Kjetil, as terrifying as Kjetil was. If this man wanted to take revenge for the driver, it would be a very big fucked up problem indeed.

4

Burly police officers cuffed Blackwood's hands behind his back and smashed his face into the concrete.

"Du er arrestert, forstår–"

"I'm English," Blackwood said.

"Du... do you understand? You are under arrest."

Another officer barked out his rights to him in Norwegian anyway. The industrial estate was now a grim procession of black-clad cops under blue lights.

A voice shouted out a command. A woman's voice.

Whatever it was that had been said, the officers reluctantly complied and yanked Blackwood back onto his feet. His face still ached from where it had been slammed against the floor. He looked up.

The woman standing before him was in her late-thirties, chestnut hair falling around her shoulders. She was dressed in a crisp, navy suit with a regulation issue puffa jacket over it.

Blackwood's eyes met hers for a moment, before she turned away.

She was tall, with a square jaw, her bearing that of a professional. She didn't look at him as she spoke; her glower directed just over Blackwood's shoulder.

"Detective Sergeant Larsen," she said in a clipped, efficient tone.

Blackwood nodded.

"You are under arrest for suspicion of murder," she said. "You will be taken to Stovner police station. We will discuss the facts there. Do you understand?"

Blackwood nodded again.

"This way," Detective Sergeant Larsen said.

She grabbed his arm with an unyielding grip and led him towards an unmarked car. The other officers compliantly got out of her way as she marched past them, her boots clicking on the pavement.

Blackwood climbed in the back of the car, awkward with his hands cuffed behind him, and Larsen got in the driver's seat. Another cop climbed in the back with him: too big for his uniform, wheezing at the effort, a fierce look on his face.

The drive to the station was made in silence, the only sound Larsen's fingers beating a steady rhythm on the steering wheel.

Eventually, Blackwood said, "I'm innocent. I witnessed the shooting."

Her dark eyes fell on him in the rear-view mirror, but she said nothing.

Blackwood checked the landmarks as the car cruised deeper into Oslo, trying to make sense of the place names and street signs. At last, the car pulled into the parking lot of Stovner Police Station. Larsen jumped out and marched towards the entrance. The partner bundled Blackwood out of the car and frog-marched him in her wake.

He felt a chill cascade through his body as he stepped up the stairs to the entrance. He was in serious trouble.

The officer hustled him inside, where they processed him, emptied his pockets, took his belt and bootlaces, his bag, and marched him down a long corridor and into a small, windowless room. There were two chairs and a table in the centre of the room and Detective Sergeant Larsen indicated for Blackwood to sit.

The partner uncuffed him and Blackwood rubbed his wrists.

They both walked out and left him to wait. His thoughts raced. How the hell was he going to get out of this? The only thing he could think of was to tell the truth. But he could never tell the whole truth.

After what seemed twenty minutes but could have been longer, Detective Sergeant Larsen and the uniformed cop returned and sat opposite him. She fixed him with a cold and demanding stare and introduced herself again.

"I'm Detective Sergeant Larsen, Division of Violence and Sexual Crimes. I'm here to question you in regard to the death of Dag Engelson. Present in the interview is Detective Constable Sogge. The interview will be conducted in English, which is the language of the suspect."

"This morning at oh-three-thirty hours, officers of the Stovner department were alerted to a shooting at the Stovner industrial estate. At the scene of the crime they found the body of one Dag Engelson, a truck driver delivering a shipment of reindeer meat to Oslo. The suspect was apprehended, attempting to flee the scene of the crime. A gun was also found at the scene, dumped into the bushes. So far, we believe the suspect apprehended to be the murderer."

Both cops stared, as if expecting him to answer them.

Blackwood took a deep breath, steeling himself, and said, "I didn't murder Dag Engelson."

"Why were you in the industrial estate?" she asked, her voice hard and direct.

Blackwood noted that subtle difference between asking him why he was present at the scene of a crime and why he'd murdered someone. That was a positive in his favour.

His interrogator seemed to sense her mistake and gave out a snort of derision. "And who are you? What is your name? You have no passport or identification."

Blackwood recalled the name he was supposed to have. The name on a passport he didn't yet hold. "My name is Owen Blake," he said. "I'm an Irish citizen travelling in Europe. I forgot my papers back in Tromsø and had to arrange for them to be sent to me here in Oslo. I'm collecting them from an automated parcel locker."

"You said you were English."

"I said I speak English. I have an Irish passport."

He wondered if she would detect that his accent wasn't remotely Irish. It didn't matter. The fake passport and driving licence, if they had arrived, would confirm everything.

Detective Sergeant Larsen continued to stare at him, looking for any hint of dishonesty. After a few moments she narrowed her eyes and said, "All right. Tell me what you know."

Blackwood told her the truth, as much as he could remember. He explained that he had been hitching with Dag, whom he didn't know. They had travelled for a whole day and half the night, all the way from Tromsø. Then, to his surprise, Dag had pulled into the industrial estate, and that was when the gunshot had rung out. All of that was true. If he told the truth, he would be fine. He hoped.

"You say *surprisingly*. Why?"

"We were at the end of our journey. Only twenty minutes more. It seemed strange that he stopped."

"Did you ask him why?"

Blackwood shrugged. "I was going to but Dag had already left the cab. And... I was sleepy. You know, long journey."

Her face gave away nothing. They would have checked the manifest and would know if Dag was delivering to that place or not, but she would not give Blackwood anything that might make it easy for him. "Tell me what happened then," she said.

Blackwood sighed and described everything, even down to the teenage boy he'd headbutted and then his panic at the police sirens.

Detective Sergeant Larsen took notes as she listened. The other cop – she'd called him Detective Constable Sogge – just glared, trying to psyche him out.

When he finished explaining, Larsen dropped her pen onto the table. "You must understand that this does not look good. You were the only one there. You knew something was happening, and you ran. It all looks very suspicious."

Blackwood had no choice but to agree. "I'm innocent," he said. "I was just in the wrong place at the wrong time."

Detective Sergeant Larsen let out a wince of pain and narrowed her eyes. "We have to investigate," she said, her voice terse. "Until we have more evidence, I'm afraid you have to remain here."

They rose and left him.

Blackwood swallowed hard. He was in for a long night.

5

Blackwood was left in the interrogation room for an hour or more. A tactic to unnerve him, he reckoned. If they had anything to keep him, they would have thrown him in a cell to sleep off the night. In any interrogation situation, it was the waiting that made a person crack. The waiting and the thinking, gnawing at your resolve until you were desperate to talk, just to fill the silence. Just to get away from your own thoughts.

Eventually, Detective Sergeant Larsen returned with two paper cups of coffee. To his surprise, it was good: strong and bitter, as real coffee should be. The kind you had to grind fresh in your own press.

Also to his surprise, Larsen did not confront him with the fact that he — or rather Owen Blake — was not on any record of entering the country. Maybe they hadn't got that information yet. Maybe he'd be out of this place before that came through.

Larsen stared at him intently. "The truck carried two tons of reindeer meat. Yet the criminals left that behind. What were they after?"

Blackwood shook his head. "I don't know. I didn't understand what they were saying. Only a few words. *Nei* and *narkotika*, I understood. But something about a green locker too."

"A green locker?"

"They mentioned it a couple of times."

Larsen consulted her notes. "We checked the manifest, and there is no record of anything else being in the truck. We've also checked the truck itself, and there's nothing hidden or out of the ordinary. Whatever they were looking for must have been something small or very well hidden, because it wasn't there."

Blackwood thought back to the truck. Three of the gang members had gone straight to the back of the truck. It was almost as if they had been expecting something to be there. And they had certainly unloaded something. "So, it looks like Dag was innocent, or why shoot him for whatever it was?"

"But Dag Engelson made the stop, almost like it was a rendezvous. You said yourself it was strange."

Blackwood nodded and stroked his chin. "I thought so, but I was just a hitchhiker. I didn't know his business. I'd known him for twenty hours and we barely spoke."

Detective Sergeant Larsen sighed and leaned back in her chair. She tapped the edge of the desk with her finger for a moment, deep in thought. Finally, she spoke and asked him to again go through the entire story, starting with hitching a ride in Tromsø.

Blackwood recounted the story all over again, making it sound plausible and totally innocent, hyper aware that it *was* plausible; it *was* innocent.

He had stumbled into a crime. It was an unfortunate coincidence. Just bad luck. But then, when you existed on the fringes of society, as he did, you upped the chance of encountering that that sort of luck. While he was totally innocent in all of this, the longer he was here, the more chance they had of discovering what he'd done in Tromsø.

A uniformed cop interrupted and called Larsen out. She scowled annoyance at her interrogation being disrupted.

Blackwood sipped his coffee and thought of nothing else but the warm, cosy sensation.

When Larsen stomped back, her face was a mottled red and her lips were pulled into a tight line. Her jaw was clenched as she said, "You're free to go. For now."

Blackwood rose, not wanting to question, but unable to help himself. "Why?" he said.

"There is CCTV footage from a camera on the industrial estate. It shows everything exactly as you described it. Mr Engelson got out and conversed with the men. An argument broke out. They shot him. That was when you crawled out of the cab." She waved her hand in the air, already tired of the detail. "And all the rest of it. You were an innocent person under attack from criminals, trying to defend himself and fleeing the scene after being shot at."

She took him out and processed him, returning his phone, his bootlaces, his bag. He sat on a hard plastic bench and tied his boots. She watched him, hands on hips. He looked up when he was done and she was still glaring.

He stood and smiled warmly at her.

She did not smile back.

"I've taken your number," she said. "You cannot leave the country. In fact, you must stay in Oslo and must report back to me as soon as you have your passport."

But they were going to let him go. Did they really think they could stop him disappearing?

Blackwood nodded silently, not trusting himself to speak. He stepped out into the cold dawn, relieved to be free and breathing in the fresh air. But the feeling didn't last long.

Larsen and her partner, Sogge, followed him out. "Detective Constable Sogge will escort you to your accommodation, Mr Blake," Larsen said.

Blackwood wondered if they had put a track on his phone. It was a burner phone he could dump, anyway.

As he walked away from the police station, he could feel Larsen's gaze on him, as if she could see through him.

6

Larsen stared through the cold, sterile glass wall, arms folded across her chest. A sigh escaped her lips as she watched Owen Blake stride out into the early morning light, the door closing with a resounding click behind him. His steps were confident — a soldier's march. This release was a bureaucratic tap dance; the man was not guilty of the murder, but guilt clung to him like a cloud of cheap aftershave.

Haaken's voice cut through the hallway, authoritative and impatient. "Team, briefing room — now!"

She pushed herself away and followed the stream of officers heading towards the briefing room. The scent of coffee thick in the air, mingling with the faint odour of rain-soaked wool from damp overcoats.

Detective Chief Inspector Henrik Haaken stood at the front, commanding everyone's attention without uttering a word. He had the same stature as Owen Blake — the suspect they all talked about in hushed tones. Tall, broad-shouldered, a presence that filled the room. Sharp blue eyes pierced the crowd, his dark hair showing hints of grey at the temples. An ex-military aura clung to him, a mirror of Blake's disciplined demeanour.

Haaken's gaze swept over the assembled officers, lingering on Larsen for a moment longer than the rest. It was a look that demanded excellence and brooked no excuses. She met his eyes, giving nothing away.

"Good work this morning at the industrial estate," he began, his tone begrudgingly approving. "But remember, we have CCTV to review, suspects that are still at large, and the teenager who was involved to track down. Our only suspect is now released."

Larsen's jaw tightened. The shooting was a single jigsaw piece with nothing to connect it to. It was a disaster.

Haaken didn't pause for breath. "Today's agenda. The illegal drinking den in Ammerud, the stabbing at the Videregående school, the ram-raid on the Co-op Prix supermarket last night, four burglaries to follow up on..."

The list of crimes unfolded like a roll call of the city's daily sins. Larsen felt the weight of each one — they were more than tasks; they were stories waiting for an end.

"And then there's the matter of the art thefts," he announced, casting a stern glance across his assembled officers.

Groans echoed off the walls, and eyes rolled in unison.

"Three Munch masterpieces, vanished into thin air from a Russian gallery." Haaken's tone held an edge of urgency as he spoke of the stolen cultural treasures. "It's a political game now," he continued, "National pride is at stake."

"There's no proof they're even in Norway," someone shouted out.

"Yet," Haaken retorted sharply. "We have a tip-off that a local gang is holding the pieces. There's chatter about a shady art dealer who might be the fence."

The room's atmosphere tightened, curiosity piqued.

"Could be any gang in this city," Haaken said, his gaze sweeping over the team before it settled back on Larsen. "Except Teo Molund's, who has been under close observation. So we can at least cross that off our list. And there's more. Rune Prestegård, businessman and philanthropist, has offered a ten-million-kroner reward for recovery of the paintings."

Murmurs swept through the team, but Larsen shook her head and looked at her boots. Prestegård was nothing but a jumped-up mafia boss trying to go legit. He was probably sitting on them himself.

"Let's get to it!" Haaken's voice boomed. He glared at Larsen as if he knew her mind was on other cases, on other suspects.

Haaken's deputy, a wiry figure with eyes sharp as tacks, began distributing the day's assignments. Officers dispersed, chatter rising again like the swell of an ocean wave.

Larsen moved to her desk, thoughts already racing ahead. Stovner, this Irishman, Owen Blake, the tangled web of crime — it beckoned her, a siren call she couldn't ignore.

When a couple of sheets of paper landed on her desk, she didn't need to read it to know her morning was gone.

"Great," she murmured, thumbing through pages dense with names and places. Half the day chasing ghosts. It was the same dance — questioning street scum who'd rather spit in your coffee than offer a crumb of truth.

She longed for the crisp air outside, the pursuit of tangible leads on the shooting, and Owen Blake with his silence and secrets.

7

Detective Constable Sogge drove Blackwood out of the bleak suburb of Stovner and into central Oslo as dawn broke over the city and morning traffic gathered along the streets. The buildings were darkened and seemed to glow, lit from inside by the light of uncounted computer screens. A single bicyclist pedalled along, his white headlight no more than a speck at this distance. The city was awakening.

"Do you have a place to stay?" Sogge asked, eventually.

Blackwood shrugged. "I was going to find a cheap hotel."

"How cheap?" Sogge asked.

"As cheap as possible."

Sogge looked back at the road behind them. "If you'd said, I could have dropped you at a hostel right in Stovner. In the city it will be expensive."

Blackwood shook his head. "No. Central is good."

Sogge sighed and eventually parked up on a back street somewhere behind the central train station. It looked like a budget hotel that catered to backpackers and stag parties. Not quite a hostel but barely a hotel. The rooms would be functional with just enough comfort to sleep.

Sogge accompanied him inside and watched while Blackwood checked in. The concierge was a young Somali woman with a bored expression. When she asked for Blackwood's passport, Sogge interrupted and explained in Norwegian that this would be forthcoming. The concierge shrugged. Sogge's uniform seemed to tide things over. She handed him a swipe card and a slip of paper with the room number: 312.

Blackwood grabbed a tourist map of the city from a cardboard display stand and pocketed it.

Sogge walked out and drove off.

Blackwood went up to the third floor, alone. The room was small, spartan and smelled of mildew. It was utilitarian but would serve its purpose.

He opened the window and breathed in the fresh air, watching the morning light grow stronger. The sounds of the city were starting to rise, and he could already feel the vibrancy of the city returning to life.

He took out the tourist map and looked for the site of the crime the previous night but Stovner wasn't on it. A smaller map on the back of the pamphlet revealed Stovner was well outside the city centre. He studied the map closely, committing as much to memory as he could.

He stripped off and collapsed into the bed, exhausted yet alert. The bed was freshly made, but the sheets were thin and smelled of bleach.

He lay there for a long time, wondering what had happened to Dag Engelson and what he had been caught up in.

8

Larsen flicked through the list, a litany of gang aliases and known haunts. Her fingers paused as she glanced up.

A school photo of her son, still chubby-cheeked and wide-eyed in this frozen moment, perched on the edge of her desk. He would cringe if he knew she had this on her desk, he was all adolescent edges and eye rolls now.

Next to him, the smile of her husband, forever paused in time.

She glanced across the room to the same photograph, larger, on the wall, framed in black.

A shudder ran through her and she closed her eyes, trying not to see the pictures that came, unbidden.

But she could never not see them.

The grainy blue light of a street at night, shot from a CCTV camera high on a lamppost. A man crossed the street, just coming out of a kebab house. Bjorn. Her husband. Going back to the patrol car. A late-night stake out. Collecting food for him and his partner.

As he crossed the street, too slow, he froze. A car roared into view. Hit him. He flew into the air, spinning like a rag doll, and hit the asphalt skull first. A second car tore through the scene and ran right over him. They sped on.

Leaving him there. So still. So dead.

Other CCTV cameras around the city picked them up – a jigsaw that was pieced together over weeks – but there was no identifying them. The cars were stolen.

Joyriders. Maybe members of any one of the criminal gangs that plagued the city.

Nothing came up.

Haaken had said exactly the same thing back then. The same words as the Irish stranger. "I'm sorry, Kari," he'd said. "He was just in the wrong place at the wrong time."

Before she could settle into the rhythm of the room, Mads Sogge bustled back in, breathless. "Owen Blake is in his hotel," Sogge murmured, just loud enough for Larsen's ears alone.

"We'll get back to him," she replied. "But first we have to follow up on the Munch thefts."

"God, those stupid paintings. The country's gone mad. They're our crown jewels now when no one cared about them before."

Larsen gave a tight smile. Sogge was a philistine, much like most of the men here. But he had a point. No one had cared about the paintings before – they were just three obscure Edvard Munch landscapes that weren't even on display in the *Nasjonalgalleriet*, just hidden in the storeroom – and now they were an intrinsic part of the Norwegian soul. It was so much bullshit.

But the paintings were beautiful. A part of Munch's output that few people knew. Most people only really knew *The Scream* and nothing much else, like he was some kind of one-hit-wonder of the art world. She was one of the few people who'd actually seen the three Munch landscapes, before they'd been stolen from the Russian gallery. Twenty years ago. That summer she'd had serious ambitions to study art history at the University of Oslo. They were loaned to the *Sjælebilleder* exhibition in Copenhagen. *Soul images.* She had gazed on them for an hour, spellbound. Three winter landscapes that called to her of home and belonging.

But then she had drifted into the more sensible choice: a degree in Criminology.

"So... do we go back and talk to Owen Blake?"

Larsen blinked. She had gone far away, for how long she didn't know. She handed Sogge the first sheet of names. "This first."

"Great," he said. "Seen any priceless Munch paintings, mister gangster?"

Larsen scoffed with him. He was right. It would be a morning of sneers and derision from Oslo's criminal fraternity. But somewhere among the lies, maybe a shard of truth might glint. "You get to it. I have to write my report about this morning."

Sogge bundled off and she turned her attention to the report. The shooting demanded clarity, precision. Every detail mapped out could mean the difference between catching a killer or letting them slip through the cracks like smoke. It struck her that one of the gangsters they would question about the stupid paintings today would be the murderer of Dag Engelson, and they would be no nearer to catching him.

The screen blinked, a blank page awaiting her findings.

She plunged into the narrative of that morning, the chaos distilled into bullet points and observations. Larsen's mind worked methodically, stripping away the noise, focusing on the facts. If luck was on her side, thirty minutes would see the end of it. Then she could be out on the streets for four hours of rough voices and hard stares greeting her inquiries.

Then she could chase up Owen Blake.

She typed, each keystroke a step closer to the door and the damp chill of Oslo's underbelly.

9

Martin cowered in the back seat as the car glided out of Grünerløkka down the Fv4 towards Middelalderparken, thick gunnels of snow slush piled in the gutters all along.

Kjetil was rambling, his brain wired from the line of coke he'd taken as a livener just before they'd set off. "It's just a threat. A show of strength. No one's going to get shot. You hear?"

He didn't wait for Martin to answer.

"You make up for botching the Stovner job with this. Show us you know how to handle a gun. Just threaten them. Show the gun. That's all. That will be enough. These small-time gang members only pack knives. Some of them are nothing but petrol bomb throwers. That's all. They run home crying to their mothers when you take out a gun. That's real life."

The other gang members in the car laughed.

Martin handled the pistol on his lap like it was a cobra, ready to strike at any time. He had been trained by his father in gun handling, but that was five years ago and he was far from an expert. He tried to keep from shaking as he kept repeating to himself, *it's just a show of strength. No one will get hurt.*

Kjetil continued talking. "We give them one warning. Any resistance will be met with fire. Just show them the gun. They'll run."

Martin pushed the safety on and shoved the gun in his pocket.

Kjetil turned to him. "You ready, kid? You up for this?"

Martin nodded. "I'm ready."

The car climbed the Nylandsveien flyover that vaulted the bus station and the tracks of the Oslo Sentralstasjon and Martin's stomach churned as they descended and turned sharp left onto Dronning Eufemias Gate. If he didn't get out soon, he would throw up.

As if he sensed it, Kjetil stopped at the crossroads with the Ring 162.

The blue tram rattled along beside them. Martin looked out at the normal people going about their normal, safe, everyday lives.

On the lights, a green arrow pointed ahead and a red arrow pointed right as if warning him.

"Get out," Kjetil said.

Martin was surprised for a moment. He'd thought they would drop him closer to the park.

A horn beeped behind them.

"Now!" Kjetil yelled.

Martin stumbled out of the car, his feet slipping on the ice. He was about to dash across the road between the cars when Kjetil called out. "Don't be afraid, Marti. Show us what you can do."

Kjetil sped off and a stream of cars followed behind him.

Martin gulped and nodded. He was still afraid, but Kjetil's words had pushed him forward. The lights turned red and Martin sped across to the safety of the corner. He waited for the lights to turn again and crossed to the park side.

It was cold and snowy as he tramped along the path that edged Middelalderparken. The icy wind cut into the split skin of his nose, stinging. He crossed into the park, steeling himself against the fear creeping through his veins.

The cold gun was as heavy as an anvil in his pocket.

10

Blackwood slept for three hours, had a cold shower, changed his clothes and headed out.

Tramping the back streets of the city, he eventually found the automated parcel locker facility between a greasy spoon café and a convenience store somewhere behind the central train station. The facility was just an empty room lined with lockers, unmanned. Anyone could walk in. He took out his phone and found the message from Lola with his QR code. He held it up to the right locker and it opened for him.

The package was inside. He tore it open and took out a fresh Irish EU passport and a driving licence, each bearing the same old photo of him. Lola had done a sterling job.

This was his VIP invite to the whole of Europe.

He was Owen Blake.

He pocketed his passport and driving licence and left the parcel locker facility. His stomach grumbled and he realized he was hungry. The small diner next door served simple, greasy food. He took a table in the corner and ate a plate of ham and eggs in silence, leaning over the table and eating the food quickly. He didn't want to linger.

A shadow fell over his plate and he looked up to see Detective Sergeant Larsen take a seat opposite. She was wearing a black jacket and a white shirt, her eyes narrowed with fatigue. Unlike him, she had not showered and changed, nor even slept a little.

"What's the food like? It looks awful."

"It's fuel," he said.

Outside, through the condensation on the windows, Sogge leaned on the hood of his police car.

Larsen held out her hand. "I see you've received your papers."

Blackwood wiped his mouth, pushed his plate away and dug into his jacket pocket to pull out the passport and driving licence.

Sogge came in, took them and went back out to his police car. Larsen hadn't even looked at them. Sogge would be running a check on their validity. They would check out, Blackwood was certain. The contact he'd given to Lola always provided top quality fake I.D.

"You know, I'm curious," Detective Sergeant Larsen said, "as to why your passport and ID are being sent to you from the UK, when you said you forgot them in Tromsø."

Blackwood thought a moment. He was impressed and had clearly underestimated Larsen. He might be one step ahead of her, but he could feel her hot breath on the back of his neck.

"Did I say that?" Blackwood replied. "No, my documents were destroyed in a fire so had to be replaced."

He looked at Larsen as she watched him, her gaze unwavering. She said nothing.

"Do you think I'm a criminal?" he finally asked.

"No," she replied. "I think you're involved in something way bigger than you know."

Blackwood nodded and looked away, glad that the little dance was over. He knew whatever he said, Larsen wouldn't believe him until he gave her proof.

With a deep breath, he looked out of the window. Sogge was still there.

For now, the game was on.

"You know," Larsen said, with a sudden tone of understanding, "we've heard whispers of something bigger going on here. Something far more dangerous than a bungled reindeer meat theft. And I know there's something more to you, Mister Blake. If that's your real name."

Blackwood chuckled. "Like I said, I was in the wrong place at the wrong time."

Her eyes blazed with sudden anger. "No one is ever in the wrong place at the wrong time. No one who can handle himself like you."

Of course, they had seen the CCTV footage of him taking out the youth and snatching his gun. All too professional. He went to say he was ex-army but held his tongue. That kind of thing could be easily checked, and Owen Blake did not have a service record.

"I know how to handle myself," he said. "There's nothing wrong in that."

Outside, Sogge climbed out of the car with a weary expression and crossed the street holding Blackwood's papers.

Blackwood couldn't help smiling. They had checked out.

"Like I said," Larsen said. "You must not leave, for the time being. I will be keeping an eye on you."

"I have no doubt," Blackwood said.

Larsen took the passport and driving licence from Sogge and handed them back. She stood, adjusted her jacket, and nodded. "Good luck, Mr. Blake." She walked out, her heels clicking on the tiles.

Blackwood watched her leave. He knew she would be keeping an eye on him and knew he had to stay alert. He was a pawn in their game, whatever that was. He had no idea how he was going to get out of this. He only knew he had to. So he finished his breakfast, paid his bill and left the diner. It was time to find out what was really happening.

11

Back in his cramped room, Blackwood sat on the bed and used the hotel Wi-Fi to scour Facebook, LinkedIn, and the Norwegian White Pages, looking for Dag Engelson. He got it down to two, but when he saw the neighbourhood next to the apartment number and street name, he knew which one it was.

Grünerløkka.

It all made sense now. They hadn't been talking about a *green locker* at all. It had been a district of Oslo.

It was only a short walk away too.

Outside, the city was dappled in grey and the light had an eerie feeling to it. He felt like he was being watched. He walked slowly, for all the world looking like a tourist taking a stroll, pausing to look in shop windows and check the reflection to see if he was being followed.

Every cop who passed by seemed to be looking at anything and anyone but him.

Detective Sergeant Larsen was either very good at her job, or she had given up.

He eventually found the apartment, a block of twenty flats above a row of shops. He sat outside on the steps for a few minutes, now less worried about being followed — no-one was here. No sign of cops or even a plain-clothes tail. It didn't matter anyway. He was visiting Dag Engelson's widow or partner. There was nothing wrong with that.

He entered the building, followed signs to the top floor and rang the buzzer.

He waited, looking at the security camera.

Nothing happened.

He rang again, this time more insistent.

Nothing.

He sighed and leaned against the door, his head thumping with frustration. What if he'd got it wrong? What if it wasn't Dag Engelson's flat?

He was about to give up when he heard the clunk of locks from the other side. The door opened with a creak and a short woman stood in the doorway looking at him with a question in her eyes. Her once-blonde hair was streaked with grey and she wore a simple dress. Her posture was stoic, her eyes heavily ringed from crying.

"Ja? Hva vil du?"

Blackwood composed himself and smiled.

"My name is Owen Blake. I've come about Dag Engelson." He saw her eyes widen. "I was with him last night, when..."

"I know who you are," she said, her voice soft and sad. "Come in."

She led him inside and told him to take a seat. He felt like an intruder in her private grief, but he stayed.

"They said he had an Englishman with him. A hitchhiker. They asked if I knew anything about you. My name is Gunilla."

She held out her hand.

He shook it and said, "I'm so sorry for your loss."

She sat down opposite, looking at him with a mixture of anger and sadness. "Dag was my husband..." Tears streaked her cheeks and her voice shook. "He wasn't involved in anything dangerous. How could this happen?"

Blackwood hesitated, not knowing what to say. Finally he said, "Was Dag in any trouble? Was there anything you can think of for why this might happen?"

She shook her head and sobbed with guttural cries that were almost animal.

All he could do was watch and wait for the wave of grief to subside.

Finally she talked, twisting a paper handkerchief in her bony hands, tearing it to shreds. "Dag was receiving cash payments. Large sums of money. I don't know from where. He said he was winning on football bets. Pah. He had never won anything before with his football knowledge, so how came it that he was suddenly so lucky? And it didn't make him happy. You would think he would be happy, to be winning all the time. But he was always so distant, paranoid. I had no clue as to who was paying him. Or why. That was what made me the most scared. I should have done something. I could have saved him from his own foolishness."

Blackwood expressed as delicately as he could. "Was he the type to get involved in foolishness?"

She shook her head, choked and then nodded, unleashing another torrent of sobs that wracked her body.

Blackwood took it all in and tried to console her by patting her shoulder and making sympathetic noises, but he couldn't feel her grief. He didn't even know what he was doing here.

"And dear God, our son is missing too. I've tried to call him so many times. What am I to do?"

"How old is your son?" Blackwood asked.

"Seventeen," she said. "He's been hanging with bad people. Always around the Middelalderparken. I keep telling him off about it, but... he's like his father."

Blackwood pondered this and said, "Can I see a picture of your son?

12

Martin looked around for any signs of the gang, but it seemed quiet.

An elderly couple walked their dog and a group of children played in the snow. Everyone too busy to look his way.

He walked on along the narrow strip of park, tramping down the pathway that had been sanded, his boots crunching on the grit.

As the park ran out, he blew a snort of relief. The rival gang were not there. He could return to Kjetil and saying they were gone and how could he threaten someone who wasn't there?

Then, as he came out to where the park gathered in a teardrop shape, he finally spotted them: a couple of youths hanging out on the old church ruins. The unmistakable careless slouch of dealers, radiating an air of menace that told anyone, whether dog walkers or snowmen-building children, to stay clear.

Martin quickened his steps, his heart pounding. He clenched his fist and touched the pistol in his pocket. Taking a deep breath, he tried to walk with an air of confidence.

As he advanced, the gang members stopped and stared at him.

One of them moved, and the other followed, stepping closer.

Martin stared at his feet and scurried past them. Their hard stares followed him as he strode on, cursing himself under his breath. He crossed the footbridge over the lake, heading out of the park. Someone bumped into him, making him gasp. A burly man all in black with a beanie hat, walking on into the park.

"Watch it," the man growled behind him.

Martin stopped, gripping the gun in his pocket again.

He should go back. Go back and show this gun to those youths. Just show them. That was all it was. A show of strength. No one had to die.

He spun around, his face hot and his heart racing. He walked back over the footbridge, steeling himself against the fear.

The man he'd collided with had veered off the path and was striding across the snow, heading straight for the boys.

The tall one stepped forward and yelled, "What the fuck do you want, old man?"

The old man took something from his pocket.

Four shots rang out and echoed across the park. A pair of vicious double cracks.

The youths fell in the snow.

Martin's legs turned to water. He couldn't move.

The old man turned and his cold eyes met Martin's through the spires of steam rising from the breathless air.

Martin turned and bolted into a run.

Something zipped past his left ear and a gunshot echoed a moment later.

He sprinted, desperate, his heart in his mouth.

Something chimed at his feet like a thrown coin and another shot echoed behind him.

Over the footbridge, ducking as he sprinted, he broke through the line of trees that skirted the path and ran along. The chicken wire railway fence barring his way.

A train clattered past, deafening.

Another shot skimmed by his shoulder and rang on the fence.

The Sørenga bridge was up ahead, a set of iron stairs leading up to a bridge that ended mid-air.

The railway fence was only the height of his head. He ran and vaulted over, hopping and jumping over the tracks, crunching gravel.

The old man in black emerged from the park, caught sight of him and fell to a crouch, taking aim.

A train parked up in a siding ahead.

Martin ran for it and scrambled behind it just as the driver's window shattered.

He sprinted for all his might along the length of the stationary train, glancing behind in blind panic.

The black figure stepped out from the train and raised his weapon.

The gun. The gun in his pocket.

Martin dived to the floor as a shot zipped by him, and in one fluid motion snatched the gun from his pocket, snipped off the safety and squeezed the trigger.

The man shrank back behind the cover of the train.

Martin didn't wait to see if he came out again.

He ran for his life.

13

BLACKWOOD FELT A PANG of guilt as Gunilla pushed herself up and ambled over to a shelf where she took down a framed photo. She passed it to him, still sniffling.

A school graduation portrait of a teenage boy. He had expected to see the face of the boy he'd headbutted last night. But it wasn't. Of course it wasn't. Dag's son wouldn't have been involved in killing his father. He felt relieved in that moment, at least. He took out his phone and snapped a picture.

"If you want, I can go look for him."

Gunilla slumped into her seat, the framed photo on her lap. She stared at her son for a moment and Blackwood thought she hadn't heard him, but she looked up with a puzzled frown, as if his offer had just seeped through her brain.

Her gaze penetrated, and it seemed she saw who he was and what he was.

"I want to know what happened to my husband," Gunilla said. "Can you help me?"

Blackwood cleared his throat. He had no idea what he was doing here, no way of knowing what had happened to Dag Engelson. But he was here, in this tiny flat, in this moment with a grieving woman who needed answers. And she sensed he could help. She had seen right through his lies about being an English hitchhiker who was just passing through. Much like Detective Sergeant Larsen had seen through it.

Perhaps he had the mark of Cain on him, and everyone saw it.

"I can try," he said. "Yes, I'll help. I'll start by looking for your son."

He would have liked to have told Gunilla that he wouldn't let her down, that he would find out what had happened to Dag and bring the people responsible to justice, whatever the cost. But he hadn't said any of that. He'd just promised to go look for her son.

"Where did you say he hangs out? A park?"

"Middelalderparken," Gunilla said.

Blackwood took out his map and asked her to point it out. She squinted at it through her tears and pointed to a tiny strip of green that cupped a line of blue lake.

"Please, bring him back to me," she said. "He needs to know what's happened to his father."

Blackwood couldn't think of anything to say. He simply nodded and left Gunilla sitting in her living room, her shoulders shaking as she silently wept. He had felt so impotent, but this was one thing he could do to help.

Outside in the fresh cold, he hardly needed to consult the folded-up paper map, or his phone. The rough outline of Oslo was imprinted on his mind.

He tramped the icy streets, enjoying the freshness of the sub-zero temperature, which was almost a deep clean of his mind.

Middelalderparken was south of the central station, out by the waterfront. He found it beyond blocks of tenement housing, a building site haunted by cranes and the clatter of train lines converging on Sentralstasjon. It was the edgeland of the city.

Blackwood surveyed the small park, a narrow strip of snow-covered grass lined with tall trees, the harsh wind whistling through the branches. He tramped down the path around the perimeter of Middelalderparken, scarcely seeing another soul.

But then he stopped dead. A gathering of police officers in black, on either side of an area that had been cordoned off with yellow tape. Someone had been killed here. He didn't need to ask.

He edged closer, cautiously, hoping to see more. One body, maybe two, were covered with a blue tarpaulin, on a patch of old ruin that looked like it was once the footprint of a church. Bodies already on the Cross of Lorraine as if ready for burial. Crime scene investigators had just arrived in their white jumpsuits, hoods and masks, looking like a ski battalion. Soon they would erect a tent to hide the corpses.

A bunch of photographers and a video camera crew stood a little off, capturing it all for the news.

Blackwood was about to turn and go back when someone called a name.

"Mister Blake!"

Detective Sergeant Larsen emerged from the crowd of police, now all fixing him with suspicious glares.

"How strange that you should be here," she said. "Two shooting incidents not fifteen hours apart and you are at both scenes. Why is that?"

"I'm guessing that the victim is Kalle Engelson," Blackwood said. "Dag's son."

"Now how would you know that?"

He took out his phone and showed her the graduation photo. "Gunilla Engelson sent me here to look for him. He's been missing since yesterday. You can check with her. I've just left her."

Larsen glanced back at the crime scene, as if figuring out the timeline and how Blackwood's alibis might check out. She might already know how long ago the shooting had happened, if there had been witnesses to it, or if the bodies were still warm.

She gave a half nod with the weary air of someone who knew it would check out, despite what she hoped. "Mister Blake, are you an ex-police officer?"

He shook his head. "Just a man looking for the truth," he said. "Do you have any leads on who did this?"

Larsen's face clouded with a frown, her eyes distant and remote. "Only you. So far."

Blackwood nodded. That made sense, in a way she didn't realize. He was the only one who could find the answers here. "So has anything like this happened here before?" he asked.

Larsen thought for a moment before deciding if she should share anything with this man. "Middelalderparken might not look much but it is another area where drug dealing gangs have moved in. We stamp them out in one part of the city and they spring up in another."

"So this might be a turf war," Blackwood said.

Larsen nodded.

"The question," Blackwood continued, "is how both a father and son have found themselves involved in this turf war and both shot dead on the same day."

"Fuck," Larsen said. "I have to go tell that woman her son is dead too."

"I'll come with you. She sent me to find her son. I said I'd find him. I feel I owe her…"

Larsen stared aghast for a second, then looked him up and down like he was a suspect in a line-up. It seemed she decided Blackwood might be useful, even if only to check his alibi with Gunilla Engelson. "I have some things to finish here," she said. "Don't run away."

She returned to the crime scene and gave out orders to the clutch of uniformed police.

Blackwood walked on, resuming his tramp around the park, his gaze not passing a single thing without scrutiny.

Someone had approached the ruins and shot Kalle Engelson. They would have either walked on north up the length of the park or more likely south, the shortest way out. He trudged the path, scanning the ground for anything that might give him a clue. The path was smudged with the footprints of a small army of police officers, so that was useless. The pristine snow on either side was better.

Something golden caught his eye. He leaned over, careful not to stand anywhere near it. About twelve inches to the side of the path, a spent bullet casing. He bent down and examined it. A 9mm.

He glanced up and down the path. The killer couldn't have shot Kalle Engelson from here as there was no clear view of the crime scene, unless the boy had run to the church ruins where the killer had caught up with him. Or this shot had been fired afterwards, walking the other way. Which meant someone had fled the scene and been shot at. A witness, or a member of the gang that Gunilla had warned him about. Her son had fallen in with a bad crowd and was always hanging about here, she'd said. Blackwood wondered how big that crowd was.

He walked on down the path and crossed a footbridge over a tiny finger of frozen lake and wandered further down along a line of trees. Here, two sets of boot prints wandered off the path and cut a swathe through the line of trees.

And here was another cartridge lying in the snow just to the side of the path.

Blackwood continued down the path till it petered out, where a strange, half-demolished bridge hung over the scene and where a fleet of police cars were parked. Keeping his eyes on the ground, he tracked back along the line of trees, back to where the footsteps had broken through.

The boot prints went straight to the short fence that bordered the rail line. Blackwood went parallel, as close as he dared, and peered over the fence, tracking a muddle of steps across the tracks leading to a train that was parked in a siding.

The driver's window was shattered.

"What do you see?"

It was Detective Sergeant Larsen. She had followed him, alone.

Blackwood nodded towards the train. "Someone escaped this way."

Larsen grunted her agreement. "I saw you crouch down. I saw the spent shells on the way."

"So you have someone who comes and shoots Kalle Engelson."

"Two victims," Larsen said. "Each shot twice."

"Double taps?"

She nodded.

Whoever did it was trained.

"There are five shells over there at the crime scene, though."

"So, presuming he didn't miss with one, that means someone, probably a witness, stumbles on the scene…"

"And the killer turns and shoots at them," said Larsen.

"Whoever it was who was fleeing, they run down here. The killer shoots at them twice more. They jump the fence and head for the cover of that train. He shoots again, shattering the train window, and probably pursues them up the track. Let's hope they got away."

Larsen nodded slowly. "I hope so. Whoever it was saw everything and needs to be found. That's our best lead."

Blackwood wondered if there was a dead body up the tracks somewhere on the other side of that parked train. He couldn't help thinking they were looking at a desperate, probably doomed, escape attempt.

14

Blackwood watched as Detective Sergeant Larsen alerted her squad of uniformed police and CSI to the evidence of the chase they had discovered. In moments she had the rail line shut down and a phalanx of officers set off to investigate the track.

They took the bodies away and Blackwood's thoughts turned to Gunilla Engelson. Today would be the worst day of her life. The day when everything she had was taken from her. It could not get any worse. And life, from now, would never get any better.

As if she was thinking the same, Larsen came to him, her face stony. "So. You said you were looking for her son."

Blackwood nodded. "Gunilla said he was hanging around with a bad crowd in this park. That's all I know. I came straight here to look for him."

"Why?" she asked. "What's it to you?"

"I felt sorry for her," he said. "I spent 24 hours in a truck cabin with her husband and I was the last person to see him alive."

It was a lie. He wondered himself why he was here. It was more than just a mysterious desire to help a bereaved widow. No, there was something else to it. A feeling that this was his business now.

Larsen sighed and nodded. "It looks like your hunch was right," she said. "It's a turf war. And these poor boys were in the wrong place at the wrong time."

"No one's in the wrong place at the wrong time," he answered. "Isn't that what you said?"

"Well, these boys can't handle themselves like you. Come." She marched off down the path, away from the crime scene.

Blackwood followed and asked, "Where are we going?"

"I have to tell Gunilla her son is dead, and maybe try to get out of her what he was doing here. You're going to help me."

They crossed the footbridge and passed where forensics had already ringed off the spent shell casings with orange aerosol paint.

"Does this mean you trust me?"

"Not at all," Larsen said. "I'm keeping you close. I'm suspicious of any drifter going nowhere who has money to spend on a new identity."

They came to the fleet of parked police vehicles and Larsen found her unmarked car. They climbed inside and he sat in the passenger seat beside her, not in the back in handcuffs. She put the car in gear and sped off.

They drove in silence for several blocks before she said, "Do you know why I became a police officer?"

Blackwood drew a blank. He shook his head.

"There was a fellow in my father's hometown who was killed in a drive-by shooting. There were no witnesses, no evidence, just a lot of rumours and gossip. Everyone knew but no one would talk. They were all too scared. That's why I do this. To bring justice."

"It's not always possible," Blackwood said. "Bad men tend to get away with bad deeds."

"No one's ever got away from me," she said.

A moment later, she stopped the car outside Gunilla Engelson's small apartment. They rang the bell and Gunilla buzzed them in. This was the last few precious moments before her world fell entirely apart. Blackwood slowed his pace on the steps, just to give her more time.

Gunilla opened the door and saw them standing there. She had a look of hopeless resignation on her face. "Has something happened to my son?"

Blackwood nodded, dreading the moment of confirmation.

Larsen stepped forward and put her hands on Gunilla's shoulders. "There was an altercation. We found your son at the scene. I'm sorry to tell you, he's dead."

Gunilla collapsed in a sobbing heap to the floor. Larsen knelt and embraced her, a useless hug of comfort amidst her excoriating grief.

Blackwood looked away, unable to stomach it. He had enough of death, enough of sorrow. Seeing Gunilla like this made him feel hollow.

Silence hung in the air like the snow in the trees outside.

Gunilla lifted her tear-stained face from the floor. Larsen walked her inside the apartment and sat her on the sofa where Blackwood had been comforting her only an hour ago. The two women switched to Norwegian.

Even though he didn't understand a word, Gunilla's awful body-wracking sobs as she talked made a ball of anger flame across his chest. He rose and marched off down the corridor.

A plaque on one of the doors bore the name *Kalle*. He pushed inside and found himself in a teenager's room, the walls covered in pictures of film stars and footballers in a royal blue and red kit. A scarf hanging over the bed in the same colours said *Vålerenga*.

He searched the room swiftly but with care. He wasn't going to ransack the boy's room. A room she would no doubt want to keep exactly as it was left. Maybe for many years. He pulled out drawers, flipped through books and scraps of paper, checked any and all pockets of clothes that were lying around. He found nothing, nothing that gave him any indication of what Kalle had been involved in.

Nothing except a photograph. It was printed on glossy paper and showed Kalle with another boy, laughing. They were arm-in-arm and smiling into the camera as if life held no problems. In the background was a bar or a café. The sign above the place was only half visible.

...akkevik.

Blackwood left the bedroom and hovered over the two women, waiting for a break in the talk. Larsen seemed to be talking to Gunilla with such care, more like a dutiful daughter than an interrogating cop.

When she looked up at him, he held up the photograph. "Is this the other boy?"

Larsen peered and nodded. "Do you know this boy?" she said to Gunilla. "He is also dead."

Gunilla squinted at the photograph through the blur of tears. She shook her head.

Larsen spoke a rapid burst of Norwegian. Blackwood recognized only one word: *identifiren*.

Gunilla nodded, still moaning, and rose. She went off up the corridor.

Larsen waited till Gunilla was shuffling around in the next room and hissed, "What do you think you're doing, searching her son's room?"

"I want to do something," Blackwood said. "There must be a reason for this. A motive. Otherwise it's just a senseless tragedy."

"It's not your call," she spat. "Don't get in my way."

"I'm sorry," Blackwood said. "What are we doing now?"

Larsen sighed. "She has to identify her son's body. This is the part I hate the most."

Gunilla came back with her coat and boots on and they filed out of the apartment block to Larsen's car.

15

THE CORONER'S OFFICE WAS a few minutes away. It took them longer to walk to the office across pedestrianised streets and the plaza outside than to drive there.

Gunilla followed Larsen dutifully, her face vacant with the same dazed expression Blackwood had seen on bomb survivors in too many places.

Inside the coroner's office, Gunilla filled out the necessary paperwork and sat in a waiting room. Eventually, the coroner, a balding man in his fifties, came through and greeted them. "I'm sorry for your loss," he said.

Gunilla nodded, her face still emotionless.

They crossed through an inner door in the waiting area and the coroner showed them into a viewing room. It wasn't like in the TV shows, where a morgue attendant lifted a sheet from a face in a white-tiled room. This was more like a funeral parlour. Through a window a body was laid stretched out as if in repose, tasteful low lighting aimed at the face.

Gunilla walked closer, transfixed by the sight. She pressed her palm to the glass and choked a sob as she recognized her son.

The body on the bench was only a boy, Blackwood saw. Seventeen, eighteen at most. His face bore the lines of innocence, softened by death. It took a moment before Blackwood recognized him from the school graduation photo, but also it was his father's face. The same dark eyes, the same solemn expression as if engraved into his face from generations past. As if this tragedy had always been destined and all they could do was watch it unfold, helpless spectators.

The business done, Larsen guided Gunilla back out to the waiting room, where a uniformed policeman was waiting to take her home. They spoke in Norwegian and Blackwood watched, remote. He hadn't been able to prevent this tragedy. He hadn't been able to save anyone. He had failed.

He took Gunilla's hand and said, "I'm so sorry. I'll find his killer. I promise."

Gunilla gripped his fingers, as weak as a baby, and nodded, as if she still trusted him, then the uniformed cop escorted her out.

Blackwood sighed in quiet fury.

Gunilla Engelson deserved answers. And so did her son. And her husband.

"You shouldn't make promises you can't keep," Larsen said.

"Someone's got to do something. I don't intend to be nice and accommodating any longer."

"It's not your place to be anything. What do you think you can do?"

"Set some fires in the forest," Blackwood said.

"I have to warn you I'll have you arrested if I see you implicated at any more shootings. You're not responsible for truth and justice here. I am."

"Look," Blackwood said. "What you need to do is search for the source of the money. Who was paying Dag Engelson? You can talk about truth and bringing justice to those responsible. But first, you need to find out where the money is."

Larsen's phone bleeped in her hand and she answered it, snapping her name. The call was brief. She was marching out of the coroner's office before she'd hung up.

They plunged back out to the freezing cold of the city.

"What is it?" Blackwood asked.

"There is CCTV footage of someone fleeing up the train tracks. They're sending it to my tablet. It's in the car."

They tramped back to where she'd parked and both jumped in. She tapped at her tablet, holding it on her lap, and Blackwood leaned over to see.

A surprisingly clear picture came through, jerking and freezing every few seconds, but it was a pristine colour picture of the train line from only a couple of hours ago, the camera mounted above and looking out of the city. A figure came running up the track alongside a stationary train. In the distance, the blur of another figure, all in black, came out from the prow of the train and shot. The figure in the foreground ducked and stumbled and pulled out a gun and shot back. Then continued with his run, getting closer and closer to the camera till he was running right under it and it was clearly a teenage boy.

It had to be another of Kalle's gang?

Larsen let out a sharp gasp of surprise.

The footage ended. She let the tablet slide off her lap and dug out her phone. "Martin," she said. "*Hvor er du?*"

Whoever it was, they talked briefly and frantically in Norwegian before the call was over.

Blackwood noted the caller ID image on her phone screen that lingered a second before she hung up. He snatched the phone from her.

"Hey! What are you doing?"

"Who is this?"

"That's my son." She snatched the phone back.

Blackwood lowered his voice. "That's the boy I headbutted last night. In Stovner."

"No," she said. "It can't be."

"Your son? He's involved in all this."

"He can't be," she said.

She shifted the car into drive and they took off at high speed.

16

BLACKWOOD HELD ON TIGHT as Larsen put the siren on and sped along the winding city centre streets. They plunged into an underpass, heading east under the city centre and pelted along it for a good while. Eventually, they burst out into the bright white of the afternoon, heading for a neighbourhood called *Helsfyr*.

Blackwood stopped himself from joking that Larsen lived in Hell's Fire, and that was pretty much how she was driving. It wasn't the time.

They pulled up outside a grey three-storey block and Larsen was out of the car before it had even stopped.

Blackwood hurried after her as Larsen entered the block and rushed up to the second-floor landing. He followed her inside and found himself in a small lounge. Martin was tall, as tall as his mother, with the same dark brown eyes.

He looked terrified.

Larsen strode up to him and seized his arm letting out a burst of Norwegian.

Martin responded, his voice trying hard not to break.

His nose had a bloody crack at the bridge where he'd been last night. Blackwood shuddered at the thought of how easily he could have killed the boy and imagined having to explain that to Larsen when she arrived on the scene.

The boy noticed Blackwood and his eyes widened in fear.

"Hello again," Blackwood said.

He went to bolt, but Larsen held him firm and said, "It's all right. He's here to help."

Blackwood stepped forward as if to shake the boy's hand, but frisked the boy expertly, rifling through his pockets.

"Hey! Get off me!"

Blackwood pulled out a phone, a pack of cigarettes and a lighter. "Where's the gun?"

"What gun? I don't have—"

"We saw you with it, on camera!" Larsen screamed. "Where did you get it?"

"I threw it away," Martin cried.

"Did you kill those boys?"

"No!"

"You were there and you fled the scene."

Martin broke down in tears and slumped onto the sofa his head in his hands. "It wasn't me. I saw it. Another man. I saw him. He shot them both then he tried to kill me. I ran."

"That checks out," Blackwood said. "We know what happened."

Larsen went through the scenario in her head again. She nodded. However, it couldn't be the whole story.

"Did you go there to kill those boys?" Blackwood asked.

"No," Martin said. "I was supposed to scare them. Just show them the gun. No killing."

"Who gave you the gun?" Larsen asked, fighting back tears. "What the hell are you involved with?"

Martin shook his head and his mouth worked but no words came out.

Blackwood glanced at Larsen, his expression begging her to keep her tears in check.

"Take a deep breath and tell us," she said.

Martin's voice was a tremble. "Kj... Kj–"

"Tell me."

"Kjetil Bergman. I got involved with his gang. It was all money and clubs and impressing girls, you know. Just playing gangster shit. Then last night they made me go along on a job. Just pick up a consignment. It was all supposed to be cool. Then they shot the guy. Then you." – Martin looked up at Blackwood and touched his busted nose, then his words tumbled out in a flood – "This morning I didn't want to come home and let you see me like this. They pushed me into another job. Just scare these guys away from dealing drugs in Middelalderparken. Kjetil's always talking about cleaning up the city because... the cops won't... do it."

His confession ended in a pained sob.

Blackwood and Larsen exchanged a suspicious glance.

"I didn't shoot them," Martin said. "I only shot at the man who was chasing me."

Larsen sat beside her son and hugged him, squeezing the life out of him. Her son had been a whisker away from ending up on the coroner's slab, like Kalle Engelson.

Blackwood sat across from them in an armchair, watching for a while, thinking. Finally, he interrupted. "So, this Kjetil Bergman is a gangster?"

Larsen nodded. "He's part of an up-market crime gang based in Grünerløkka."

"What do you mean, 'up-market'?"

"They are borderline respectable. Run a few nightclubs. They don't get caught dealing street drugs or anything as low rent as that. They're almost moving into corporate crime."

"Doesn't sound like it."

"Kjetil is always complaining about the street gangs," Martin said. "He wants to clean up the city."

"Sounds like he wants to wipe out the competition," Blackwood said.

"He's a vicious criminal," Larsen said. "I can't believe you would be so stupid to get involved with him."

"I'm sorry," the boy said.

"The main thing is," Blackwood said, "there's a gun out there with your fingerprints. And you're on film fleeing the scene. This isn't going to end well."

"Shit!" Larsen said. "But we can prove he didn't kill those boys. The bullets won't match. We can prove he only shot back at the real killer."

"It still doesn't look good."

Larsen's phone began to ring. She answered it with a curt, "Larsen," and listened.

Whatever it was, it wasn't good. She closed her eyes and hung up.

"Fuck," she said. She turned to her son. "That was a colleague warning me. They've identified you, Martin. They're coming to pick you up."

The boy shot up as if he was going to flee once more.

Larsen shoved him back down again. "Stop! Let's think."

Blackwood rose. "Tell me where I can find Kjetil Bergman. Quickly. We don't have time."

Larsen stared dumbfounded for a moment, then put it all in place. "Yes. Tell him, Martin."

The boy blurted out an address for a nightclub and Blackwood walked out.

Larsen rushed after him down the hallway. "Wait, Owen."

He almost didn't know she was addressing him. He turned, his hand on the door latch.

"You can't do anything now," he said. "They're going to take you both in. I can help. Like you said."

She went to protest but the stark reality of their situation washed over her like a wave. "Okay. But please, no killings."

He didn't promise. He sprinted out of there and was a block away when two police cars sped past, heading for Larsen's apartment building.

17

A few streets away from Larsen's apartment block, Blackwood flagged down a taxi and gave the Yemeni driver his hotel address. An agonising twenty minutes later, he jumped out and swerved into a mini mart a few doors from the hotel. Swiftly, he rifled a packet of cooked chicken breast and a tub of cottage cheese.

Once inside his hotel room, he slumped against the wall, suddenly overwhelmed by exhaustion. He plugged in his phone to get some charge, and then did the same for himself. He'd been running on adrenaline for far too long and the crash was imminent. There was no time to grab some sleep. He scoffed down the chicken and cottage cheese, like an animal: high protein fuel to revive him, nothing more. Then he stripped off and took a cold shower, drying himself vigorously and dressing again.

He gulped down a pint of water as he sat up on the bed and figured out a plan of action. Kjetil Bergman was the key, but something about all of this didn't make sense. He looked up the nightclub on his charging phone to find everything he could. He consulted the Maps app again a little more carefully and examined what he could of the place using the satellite images and the street view. It was old info, he knew, but the best he had.

A search of the nightclub's owners found Rune Prestegård, who appeared to be a businessman with his fingers in a number of concerns. His LinkedIn profile portrayed him as a respectable businessman and supporter of the Progressive Norway Party. Lots of Twitter posts about their leader, Ingrid Borstad, parroting party slogans about cleaning up Oslo. All in English. Which made sense if you were aiming for the European business market.

Kjetil Bergman also had a LinkedIn profile but there was very little on it. Just enough to make it seem he was a nightclub manager. A convenient cover.

Blackwood took a wad of Euros from his holdall and pocketed a few hundred. It worried him that he had no transport, but the city seemed small enough and he could always grab a cab if he needed to.

The nightclub in Grünerløkka was a twenty-minute walk along icy streets. He marched at a swift pace, which kept him warm. He made it in fifteen minutes and strolled the area to align the land with the map.

It was a warren of close streets with former factory units covered in graffiti art, a bohemian arts colony sandwiched between two gentrified areas of the city. Blackwood navigated the streets carefully, his ears straining for footsteps or the sound of a car engine. When he approached the club, he ducked into a doorway to get a better look.

The club was large, an old factory unit, covered in graffiti. It faced a billboard that bore an obscenely large grinning blonde. The politician he'd seen this nightclub owner supporting. Ingrid Borstad.

To the side and along the rear of the building were steel stairways. Up on the gantry, a fire escape door was wedged open.

He skipped boldly up the fire escape as if he belonged, knowing his confidence would see him through.

Inside, he found himself looking down on a cavernous black space. A vacuum cleaner hummed down on the dance floor.

Along the upper level were numerous VIP booths and there, a lit sign on the door saying *BARE ANSATTE*. Something about it, perhaps the typography, suggested *STAFF ONLY*.

He sauntered through and found himself in a back space with an office and a couple of storerooms. The office had a couple of desks for whoever did the actual work and a few sofas clustered in a lounge area around a flatscreen TV and a games console.

Again, a now familiar face: a couple of campaign posters for Ingrid Borstad's party. *Rydde opp i Oslo.*

He tried to log into the computer but was presented with a password block. He was not a hacker. The only way he was getting away with any information on this computer was walking out with it under his arm.

He rifled the desks, poking through the contents of the drawers and logbooks on the desktops, looking for anything that would give him a lead.

But there was nothing.

On a rolodex, he found a card for Rune Prestegård with his name, address and phone numbers. He tore it out and shoved it in his pocket.

He gazed at the room. There must be something here.

His eyes fell on a poster on the wall headed *STAF*. A bunch of mugshots were lined under it, with names and phone numbers. One face caught his eye.

Martin Larsen was on a row at the bottom, all young kids. This wasn't staff; this was a list of all the boys and girls they'd groomed to be foot soldiers in their gang. On the rows above, the faces were older, meaner: a proper rogues gallery: the definition of hardened criminal. They might as well have each been holding up a prisoner number.

Blackwood took out his phone and snapped it. He had the entire gang: names, photos and phone numbers.

It wasn't so astonishing that they would be this careless. A gang like this would never expect anyone to be fool enough to walk in and take this. Even in the event of a police raid, they could claim it really was the staff list. They would all be on the payroll, even the kids.

He was almost to the door when he heard the unmistakable sound of a car engine growling closer. He darted to the window and peered down at the alley behind the club. Three men stepping out of a black Mercedes. Blackwood had no doubt who these were. Kjetil Bergman and his men.

He strode out of the office and along the corridor. He eased open the door to the upper landing of the club. Kjetil Bergman and his men were already bouncing up the stairs, cutting off his exit route.

He backed down the corridor and dived into one of the storerooms. He could hide until they went into the office, then sneak out, maybe.

But another idea gripped him.

He grabbed a cleaning cloth and a bottle of disinfectant spray and walked right out.

The three men came bowling into the corridor and stopped dead.

"Hvem er du?" Kjetil Bergman growled.

Blackwood smiled and approached. "Hi. I'm the new cleaner."

He saw their frowns as they processed this. That moment of doubt was all he needed to traverse the seven strides it took to be in range.

He sprayed a jet of disinfectant right in Kjetil Bergman's eyes.

The man screamed, buckled and stumbled back.

One of his henchmen leaped forward, but Blackwood bounced the fat disinfectant bottle off his skull.

It was too easy to grab his flailing arm, propel him on his journey and smash his face into the floor.

The man was unconscious and wouldn't get up any time soon.

The third man had already pulled a gun from his inside pocket.

Blackwood stepped into his reach, grabbed his firing arm and slammed it into the wall.

A vicious crack sounded and the man yelped in animal pain.

Blackwood slammed him at the opposite wall and his head cracked open.

Kjetil Bergman staggered blindly to his feet for a moment, only a moment, before a boot smacked him in the jaw with a sickening crack.

He buckled, legs gone, and fell in a pile of meat and bone.

All three neutralised in less than ten seconds.

Blackwood caught his breath, standing over the bodies for a moment. He snatched up the gun, a Kahr P9, a snub-nosed black number. Nine millimetre.

That was a thought.

He swiftly checked the gun. Seven in the clip, one in the spout. Fully loaded. This wasn't the gun that had shot the boys at the park. Unless Kjetil Bergman had reloaded afterwards.

Kjetil Bergman let out a moan and blinked his eyes open, trying to focus on the man who loomed above him.

Blackwood put the gun to his face.

The temptation to shoot him in the head was strong, just like this murderer had shot Dag Engelson last night.

His finger trembled on the trigger.

Larsen had said no killing.

"It's your lucky day," Blackwood said.

He delved into Kjetil Bergman's pocket and pulled out the man's phone. With that, he stepped over the bodies and made for the door, skipping down the stairs and out of the club.

Once outside again, he breathed a sigh of relief that he had made it out alive.

He marched down the street and turned onto a main thoroughfare.

As he walked, he took out his burner phone and called Larsen but there was no answer.

18

Larsen had watched Owen Blake march away down the street, the sirens blaring louder, and wondered if she'd done the right thing.

She dragged Martin out of the apartment and down the stairs.

It was Sogge who had called her to warn her. You did that for your own. There was the police force vs everyone else, but there was also Stovner station vs Oslo central, and beyond that there was your loyalty to your partner or whoever you worked with the most.

"Where are we going?" Martin cried.

She bundled him outside. "On your knees," she said.

"Why?" Martin protested.

She kneeled herself and pulled him down. "On your knees and hands up."

She held her palms up in the air and Martin copied her.

The sirens bore down on them, perhaps only two blocks away.

"Just tell the truth," she said to Martin. "Tell them everything, but especially stress how you were coerced and threatened to carry that gun. Stress that you haven't killed anyone and you have just confessed to me once I identified you."

"Okay," Martin said. His face had turned pale.

"You'll be all right."

Two police cars roared into the parking space before the apartment block.

"Oh, and don't say anything about Mister Blake. The only time you have ever seen him was last night."

Martin nodded and gulped.

"Do you understand?" she demanded.

"Yes," he said.

The police cars skidded to a halt right before them and cops jumped out.

In moments they handcuffed them and searched them and bundled them into separate cars. Her son was on his own now.

Larsen's heart ached.

Was it a heart attack or a panic attack?

She took in a deep breath and calmed herself, observing the feeling, as if floating above herself, disconnected.

No, this was a feeling she had had many times now. Only that her son was adrift and helpless. But it was really that he no longer needed a mother. That she was no longer useful.

Martin had already left her. Long ago.

They sped off, sirens blaring and strangely at odds with the serene pace of the drive. She watched the buildings pass lazily as the snow drifted down from the sky.

It was about the time his father had died. That was when Martin had become a man. Had been forced to grow up, as if he was preparing to step into his father's shoes.

Both the men she had built her life around had left her now.

As they pulled into the central Oslo police station, she steeled herself.

They uncuffed her as soon as she was inside.

"Was there any need for that?" she asked.

They looked shamefaced. They took her to an interrogation room but she strode ahead, as if she were taking them.

Before they could question her, she blurted out her account of the morning's events, as if it was her report and she was merely apprising them of a case, bringing them up to speed.

The interrogation was brief and they let her go.

"What about my son?"

"He has to answer some questions."

"He will cooperate. He will name Kjetil Bergman. This morning he was fleeing from a killer and only shot back in self-defence. "

"It's a serious crime."

"He will cooperate and lead you to the real criminals. But at the moment, his life is under threat. I want him protected. Before you release him, I want to know. If you turn him out onto the street, they will kill him. He is, as of now, a key witness."

The cops sighed. This was more than a simple collar. Much more. And this bitch from the Stovner station was somehow now in charge.

Though the cops hesitated, they did look at each other in agreement. "We'll have him witness-protected, don't worry."

Larsen nodded. It was a good start.

She walked out to the cold air. It killed her to leave her boy in that place. But all common sense told her he was safest there.

Logic didn't stop the sharp needle of pain in her chest, though.

Her mind raced through the options: taxi home and get her car, report to Detective Chief Inspector Haaken, find Kjetil Bergman, find the real killer of Kalle Engelson.

Contacting her station boss would mean a colossal delay as she'd have to go over everything again and make a statement. House of bureaucracy.

The most urgent task was finding Kjetil Bergman. That man was out there, perhaps looking for her son, the only witness to the shooting of Dag Engelson.

But to follow the lead on him, she had to report to the station.

Every option was an obstacle to saving her son.

She took out her phone to call an Uber and noticed a missed call from Owen Blake.

She cursed as it hit her.

The only way around these obstacles was Owen Blake.

How had this former soldier – he had to be – turned drifter ended up in the middle of this twisted web? And could she trust him, despite the blood on his hands?

19

Blackwood's cab sailed west through streets that became progressively more upmarket the further west from Grünerløkka they drove.

He sat in the back and scrolled through Kjetil Bergman's phone.

His photo stream revealed pictures of two boys at the Middelalderparken location. Two boys doing a deal. Surveillance photos taken on a long lens. Not taken with this phone.

He stopped at a picture of Dag Engelson hopping out of his truck on an industrial estate. A day shot. Dag meeting with a security guard. It looked like the Stovner location.

This was as good as proof. Surveillance shots that provided a direct link to murder victims. But it only proved Kjetil Bergman had surveilled the dealers in Middelalderparken. It didn't prove that he'd had them shot. And it looked very much, from Martin's account, like he hadn't. Someone else had stepped in and done that.

Dag Engelson was a different matter. Blackwood's testimony and Martin's confession would put Kjetil Bergman at the scene and firing the fatal shot.

Blackwood thought hard.

This was never going to get as far as Blackwood giving evidence, standing up in a court of law. He knew that. As soon as he could, he would take his false ID and get as far away from this mess as possible.

And that thought bothered him.

Not just because it wasn't the right thing to do, and he felt a primal compulsion to help Larsen and her son and to do what was right. But also the pure practical point now that Owen Blake, this false passport he possessed, was on the map and part of a police investigation. The only way to disappear would be to secure another passport. Unless he somehow resolved this mess and effectively disentangled Owen Blake from it.

The driver came to pull up outside Rune Prestegård's home. Not an apartment block but a stately stand-alone townhouse ringed by a decorative wrought-iron fence.

"Drive on," Blackwood said.

The Yemeni driver nodded. He more than likely understood English. Like most migrant workers in Europe, he probably spoke four or five languages.

They drove round the corner and Blackwood handed him a 200 kroner note and told him to keep the change.

He walked around the block, checking access points and discovered the best way in was to the rear. A brick wall only head height and screened by a row of firs would give him easy access to the rear garden.

He stalled for a while, pretending to check his phone. Just a guy who'd stopped to tap out a message.

Then his phone purred and Larsen's name flashed on the screen.

He stopped himself answering with his real name. "Black— Blake."

"Owen," she said. "Where are you?"

"Uranienborg. I'm about to call on Rune Prestegård."

"What the hell?" She sounded like she was in a moving vehicle. A radio playing. As she hadn't turned the radio on in her own car, and as it wasn't the occasion to be listening to the radio, he could only surmise she was in a taxi. The police would have taken her in with her son, and she was now going home to get her car.

"His name has come up as being connected to all of this," Blackwood said. "So I'm about to do some snooping."

"Listen," she said, her voice taking on a close resonance as if she'd shielded her mouth. "This person is a high-ranking mafia boss. He runs the city's underground gambling circuit."

"And you've never arrested him."

"He's untouchable. He has the sheen of respectability, and highly paid lawyers who keep him safe. I have always suspected there are people in high office protecting him."

"Would this be a certain politician named Ingrid Borstad?"

"What? Her? No. She's nothing."

"He's a huge fan of hers. What does *Rydde opp i Oslo* mean?"

"Clean Up Oslo," Larsen sneered. "You'd think that would be the last slogan a mafia boss would get behind."

"In my experience," Blackwood said. "Politicians tend to pick the slogan that's the opposite of their intentions."

"You need to be careful."

Blackwood smiled as a police car sailed past. Whatever had happened with her son, she was no longer telling Blackwood to keep out of it. He was no longer her prime suspect. That was good enough. "I'll be discreet. I promise."

"Listen," she said. "I have to call in, and that will involve some... bullshit. But I beg you, don't do anything extreme."

"You call in and do what you have to do," Blackwood said. "This is my way of helping."

The sound of the cab's motor throttled down in the background. "Thanks," she said. "Good luck."

It made him smile. "Roger that," he said.

He pocketed his phone and noted the time. A scan of the street confirmed all was clear and no one was observing him from the apartment block opposite. He vaulted the wall and landed in a flower bed. Motionless, he stood at the foot of the garden, observing the house. No lights at any of the windows.

He crept up the garden, making his way to the huge French windows. Beyond them a capacious dining area and white show kitchen.

He pulled out a penknife and prised it into the gap between the large French windows. It was surprisingly easy to jemmy open. But then, men like Rune Prestegård thought their reputation was security enough.

He slipped into the enormous kitchen and crept through to a great open hallway with a marble tiled floor and a majestic marble staircase that curved up to a balcony.

To his left, though, was a door to an great living room space, minimal and tastefully designed, almost like an art gallery. Except the pictures that hung on the wall were kitsch. They weren't exactly dogs playing poker but were not much better, even to Blackwood's untrained eye. Certainly not the kind of classy art you would expect in such an interior.

Blackwood scoffed. A gangster could buy the best of everything, but they couldn't buy taste. Unless this kind of schlock really was the thing right now.

He checked behind the pictures for a safe but found nothing but white wall.

Outside, he crossed the chequered floor and scooted up the marble steps to the upper storey, a long corridor lit by the giant skylight.

Finally, he stopped in front of the door at the end of the landing.

He put his ear to the door, trying to listen for any sound from the other side.

Silence.

He turned the handle and let himself in.

A large room, sparsely furnished in an attempt at minimalism that looked soulless, clinical.

There were several other bedrooms with en-suite facilities. The place was almost a hotel. An empty hotel.

There was one last room at the end of the landing. He took a deep breath and stepped inside.

It was large and spacious, with an old-fashioned, rather military flair to the interior decor. And it was definitely an office.

But the great walnut desk that dominated the room was totally bare. He opened the drawers to either side but they were empty. It was nothing but a showroom: the idea of a rich man's study. In fact, the whole house seemed to be nothing but a showroom. If it wasn't for all the clothes in the walk-in wardrobes and the food in the enormous fridge, you would think no one lived in this house at all.

Blackwood examined the edge of the desk and pulled at a lever which would be at your belly if you were sat at the thing.

A hidden compartment slid out revealing several items sitting on blue baize. There were four mobile phones arranged in a neat row. And a slim silver laptop which was almost a sheet of glass it was so thin.

He opened the laptop and the screen flashed to life, revealing a series of surveillance photos. It must have been the last thing Rune Prestegård looked at before he put the laptop away.

Blackwood flicked through the photos. The same surveillance photos as on Kjetil Bergman's phone: the two boys at Middelalderparken, doing their deals with various punters, the shots of Dag Engelson on the industrial estate.

There were also pictures of Detective Sergeant Larsen at the Middelalderparken crime scene. From only a couple of hours ago. What he'd thought was a press photographer had been a plant.

And then, Blackwood's heart went cold.

A photo of himself stepping out of the Stovner police station and pausing on the steps.

He closed the laptop and tucked it down the front of his jeans, zipping his jacket over it.

He didn't know what constituted evidence of collusion in murder, but maybe this was something.

Rune Prestegård, the untouchable mafia boss, had been the one who had orchestrated the hit on the

Middelalderparken boys. He had been the one who had orchestrated the hit on Dag Engelson, and Blackwood had unknowingly walked into the middle of the assassin's playground.

With this knowledge, Blackwood could now spare Larsen the ordeal of facing an unrelenting criminal trial. He had the proof he needed and all that remained was to figure out a way to deliver it to the authorities.

He marched out of the office.

Standing in the landing, barring his way, was a man.

And in the man's hand was a gun, pointing at Blackwood's heart.

20

LARSEN PULLED HER CAR into the Stovner station parking lot. The tires crunched on the grit and ice. She eased into an empty space between two other vehicles and sat with her head resting on the steering wheel for a moment. How was she was going to explain this to her boss?

She punched in and walked to her desk.

Sogge emerged from the kitchen with a mug of coffee and stopped dead, shooting a look of concern. She tried to smile and was going to thank him for his warning. If he hadn't sent her the footage, she might not have been able to save her son. But before she could get to him, Detective Chief Inspector Haaken beckoned her into his office with a wave of his hand.

"What in God's name has happened today?" he barked.

"The Middelalderparken murder has taken a major step forward." As she said it, she barely believed she'd opted for that tack.

"Your *son?*" Haaken said.

"He's a witness to the murders and is under police protection."

"He's involved in the Stovner industrial estate murder!"

"He's an innocent boy who's been groomed by Kjetil Bergman's gang, probably to get to me, but he is now turning state's evidence."

Haaken shook his head and looked at the carpet, defeated. "I can't shield you from this."

"From what?" Larsen asked, a rising swell of fear knotting in her throat.

"I'm sorry," he said.

He walked out, beckoning her to follow, and guided her to one of the interrogation rooms. Inside, a man and a woman sat waiting.

She knew they were *Spesialenheten* — Internal Affairs — before they introduced themselves.

The man rose and reached out to shake her hand. "Detective Sergeant Larsen. I am Detective Sergeant Olav Volden of the Norwegian Bureau for the Investigation of

Police Affairs, and this is my colleague, Detective Inspector Maria Westrum."

Larsen shook their hands and sat at the desk, pushing her chair out so she appeared aloof. She crossed her legs, her boot pointing at the door.

"For the sake of the recording," Olav Volden continued, "Detective Chief Inspector Henrik Haaken is also present."

The red light up by the security camera glared, a beady eye that saw all.

"Of course," Volden said, "you have the right to a defence lawyer, if you—"

"I'm fine," Larsen said.

"And you have the right to—"

"I know my rights," Larsen snapped, unable to hide her smirk. "Just get on with it."

Volden opened a card folder and read from a sheet of type. "This morning a suspect was arrested in the matter of the murder of two male victims, suspected drug dealers, at Middelalderparken. The suspect was caught on security camera fleeing the scene and discharging a pistol."

"Shooting at the murderer who was pursuing him," Larsen interrupted. "Shooting in self-defence."

"This suspect, it has emerged, is the son of Detective Sergeant Kari Larsen. Martin Larsen. And it has emerged that Detective Sergeant Larsen became aware of his involvement and did not alert the authorities."

"That's not true," Larsen said. "I found him and handed him in to Oslo Central."

"Detective Sergeant Larsen was apprehended with her son when officers from Oslo Central came to arrest him."

"I was not arrested. I made sure my son was taken into custody and that he would cooperate. He has been groomed by a criminal gang well known to us and is now turning state's evidence. I ensured that happened."

Volden glanced at his colleague. Something passed between them. Of course, Detective Inspector Maria Westrum, as the senior officer, was in charge, but she had said nothing so far.

Volden continued. "There is also the matter that Martin Larsen is identified as involved in the Stovner industrial estate murder last night."

Larsen's heart thumped. "I can explain the circumstances."

Maria Westrum shook her head and finally said something, her voice a velvety croak. "We have evidence that suggests you were colluding with the prime suspect, an Irish national called Owen Blake, to cover up the murder, to keep your son safe."

"That isn't true. Mister Blake was a suspect, but CCTV footage proved that he was not the shooter and merely protected himself. He has been helping us with our enquiries into the incident."

"We have a photo of you speaking to Mister Blake at the Middelalderparken crime scene."

"Again, Mister Blake is helping us with our enquiries."

"Into both incidents?" Volden asked.

"They are connected."

"Via your son."

"Via Kjetil Bergman's gang. It was his gang that shot Dag Engelson at the Stovner industrial estate. My son was there and witnessed it. And it was Kjetil Bergman who sent my son to Middelalderparken, with a gun, to scare the dealers that operate there."

"And they were both shot," Westrum said.

"By another suspect, who then tried to shoot my son."

"That isn't at all clear."

Larsen felt the walls close in around her. She had to fight her instinct to run. "It's not what it looks like," she said, trying to keep her voice level.

Maria Westrum leaned forward, her expression softening. "We believe you, Detective Sergeant Larsen. We know you were just trying to protect your son. But we still have to investigate this thoroughly. And we need to know if there's anything else you're not telling us."

Larsen nodded, her eyes cast down. "I do just want to keep him safe," she said. "But I also turned him in."

The woman gave her a reassuring smile. "We understand."

Larsen let out a long breath, relieved.

"But," Volden said. "You will, of course, be suspended from duty while this investigation takes place."

"What? You can't do that."

Detective Chief Inspector Haaken, sat in the corner, nodded sadly. It had already been decided.

"I'm afraid we must," Maria Westrum said.

Larsen's stomach dropped as the weight of the situation hit her. She looked down at her hands, still shaking slightly from the shock of what had happened. "I understand. I'll go home and have nothing to do with any police matters."

Volden nodded in agreement and Haaken gave her a sympathetic look.

Larsen walked out to the office space, heading for the exit but couldn't resist glancing over at her colleagues. Sogge rose from his desk and gave a questioning look.

She nodded to him and threw a brief smile of thanks.

As she walked out to the cold outside, the thought hit her: that she had abandoned everything she had worked so hard for — her career and her team — in order to protect her son.

She tramped across a patch of gritted ice to her car and set off for Uranienborg.

21

Blackwood froze, his heart pounding in his chest.

Rune Prestegård was a lean man with closely cropped grey hair and piercing green eyes. He wore a sharply tailored navy Lazio suit.

Blackwood noted all of this in an instant. But it was the gun pointed right at Blackwood's heart he noticed the most.

Two burly men flanked Rune Prestegård, not as well tailored, and thick and muscly under their suits, like bouncers at this art gallery of a home. One was bald, the other sported a sharp blond flat top.

Prestegård said something in Norwegian.

"Sorry," Blackwood said. "You speak English?"

"It is customary to knock when one is making enquiries."

They thought he was police. They had a photo of him stepping out of Stovner police station. But surely, if their surveillance was so great, they'd seen him arrested and taken in in handcuffs.

"I can go and get a search warrant," Blackwood said, and moved to push past them.

Prestegård stepped back and the heavies took his place in a heartbeat. Flat Top punched Blackwood in the guts with a fist like a ham hock.

It was the kind of punch that would leave any man crawling for breath through a pool of his own breakfast.

But the man howled and snatched his broken hand back.

Blackwood right-hooked him into the wall.

The man crumpled, leaving an imprint of his shoulder in the plaster.

Baldy blundered forward and Blackwood met him with a headbutt that splattered his nose across his face.

"You seem to be forgetting this," Rune Prestegård said.

The gun. Raised to eye level. Just out of reach.

Rune Prestegård smiled politely. "Please. Be my guest."

He nodded to the room behind and Blackwood backed up, his hands in the air.

The heavies scrambled to their feet and lumbered into the room. In an instant, they pulled Blackwood onto an office chair and Baldy cable-tied his hands behind his back.

Flat Top made an effort to frisk Blackwood's pockets, one-handed, still wincing in pain. He relieved him of his wallet, passport and phone, which he placed on Prestegård's desk. But he missed the gun. Blackwood pushed his haunches deeper into the chair to feel the Kahr P9 pistol tucked into his waistband.

Finally, Baldy, his face a giant splodge of blood, unzipped Blackwood's jacket and pulled out the laptop. Its smooth silver surface now rumpled with a giant dent.

Prestegård sneered with disgust, sat at his desk and leafed through the passport.

Finally he regarded Blackwood with an unreadable expression.

"Mister Owen Blake. Who are you? What do you know about me?"

Blackwood was silent. Any answer he gave might cost him his life. But also Prestegård had a photograph of him coming out of the police station. How much did he know about his connection to Larsen and the botched Middelalderparken investigation?

"I don't know what you're talking about," Blackwood said, trying to stay calm.

Prestegård stepped closer and glowered down at him. His face was a mask of anger but his eyes were cold and calculating.

"What are you doing here?" he growled.

"Sightseeing," Blackwood said.

The punch blinded him for a moment. He reeled and the chair, on coasters, rolled to the side. The one with the shattered hand pushed him back into place.

Prestegård gave a small, humourless laugh. "Don't play games with me. I know you're connected to Larsen. So tell me, how are you involved?"

Blackwood thought quickly. He had to come up with something convincing if he was going to survive this encounter. "I was hired to find out what happened to the boys at Middelalderparken," he said. "And it brought me to you."

"But I have nothing to do with that unfortunate incident."

"That's not what the photos on your laptop say."

Prestegård's eyes narrowed to slits, as if he were thinking hard. "It is true. I have had the situation monitored for some time. But I did not have those boys shot."

"You sent Detective Sergeant Larsen's son to kill them. You've been grooming him to do your dirty work."

Prestegård considered this as if it was new information he'd never heard of. "It might be that one of my men asked the boy to go and scare them. They are a stain on the community, you see. A problem that needs sweeping away."

"They're competition," Blackwood said.

"One might view it so. But it remains that I did not have them shot."

Blackwood mulled this over. It was clear this was true. They'd sent Martin to scare the boys, but at the same moment someone else had come and shot them. There was another agent at play here.

"Sure. You're just an honest businessman, aren't you?"

Prestegård stepped closer and fixed Blackwood with a menacing stare. "You should mind your own business, Mister Blake. This is all rather above your pay grade."

Blackwood faced Prestegård down with a steady gaze. "Call the police," he said calmly.

A muscle twitched in Prestegård's jaw and he seemed to be considering his options. After a moment, he stepped back and gave an almost imperceptible nod to his men. And with that, all three men left the room.

Their heavy footsteps sounded on the stairs and disappeared down the hallway.

Blackwood listened to them tramp away with a sense of relief.

They were not going to call the police.

What would they do – kill him and dump his body somewhere?

He perhaps only had about two minutes.

He tugged at his cable-tied binds but it was no use, they were too tight and he couldn't loosen them. There was only one way. He pushed himself up and out of the office chair so he was standing with his hands still tied behind his back. Shimmying his hips he worked his bonded wrists down over his buttocks and squirmed one leg out of the loop. Gasping and sweating, he worked the other leg out till his hands were before him.

Now for the hard part.

He bit the loose part of cable and pulled them tighter till his wrists stung with the pain. He pushed his fists behind his head, took a couple of deep breaths, readied himself, and thrust his fists forward over his head and out.

The ties snapped and the loop of cable flew across the room.

He rubbed his wrists and looked around the room.

The window.

He opened one of the panes and peered out. It was a fifteen-foot drop to the rear garden, with a great hawthorn tree obscuring the way, and a concrete patio below, but he had no other option.

He grabbed his wallet, phone and passport, and snatched the dented laptop, shoving it down his jeans again.

He climbed onto the window, took a deep breath, and jumped.

He crashed through branches and smacked onto the concrete with a thud. As his feet hit the ground he rolled forward and sprang up to a shooting position, pulling out the Kahr P9.

Prestegård and his men stared dumbfounded from the kitchen.

Blackwood squeezed the trigger.

The whole rear panorama window shattered and fell like an iceberg sliding into a lukewarm sea. Prestegård and his men took cover.

Blackwood sprang to his feet and ran.

The twenty yards of garden he'd casually strolled only minutes ago were now the length of a football pitch.

He heard them shouting behind him.

Something zinged past his ear and a shot boomed out.

Blackwood leaped for the wall and vaulted it, almost landing headfirst into the street behind. Battered, he staggered to his feet and tried to hobble away.

They would run to the wall and come over and shoot him dead. It would take seconds. He could not run for cover.

A car came hurtling at him. The horn blared. It skidded to a halt with a shriek right alongside him. The passenger door flew open.

Larsen shouted, "Get in!"

He fell into the car and she sped off with the passenger door flapping.

22

Larsen drove hard, heading south away from the rarified streets of Uranienborg, her eyes more on the rear-view mirror than the road ahead.

For the third time, Blackwood said, "No one's following."

Finally, she heard him and her shoulders sagged.

She pulled off the road and parked outside an American themed diner. Not the fake Hollywood kind, all white with red vinyl seats and a ton of chrome; more the kind you might actually walk into in the 1950s, low lit, with cosy walnut panelling and brown Naugahyde booths.

Blackwood followed her inside and sat across from her in a window seat booth. The Kahr P9 pressed cold in the small of his back. He wouldn't let Larsen know about it. Not until it was absolutely necessary.

A waitress came and Larsen ordered in rapid Norwegian.

Before the waitress returned with two coffees, Larsen told him about her suspension. He filled her in on all the details of his morning.

"So you beat up Kjetil Bergman and his gang at the *GladHus* nightclub and then burgled Rune Prestegård and assaulted his bodyguards. That wasn't very discreet."

"You said no killing. They're all still alive."

"I should have kept you in custody."

"If you had, you'd still be suspended and you'd know nothing about Rune Prestegård's involvement with your son."

She sighed and wrung her hands. "So tell me. What evidence do you have?"

Blackwood pulled out his phone and showed her the photographs. "At the nightclub there's a staff roster. Your son is on it. As are a number of other kids and some guys who look like they might have been through the prison system. I'm sure you can ID them."

Larsen pinched the photo to close-up and swiped around it, first focussing on her son's face, then on the others.

"They're definitely not the nightclub staff. And that's where I got Prestegård's address."

"So you broke in."

"I don't think Prestegård ordered the hit on the Middelalderparken boys, but I'm pretty sure he orchestrated the hit on Dag Engelson."

"How do you know?" Larsen asked.

Blackwood took out the laptop and pushed it across to her. The sleek silver dented by the imprint of Baldy's fist. "He has a ton of surveillance photos of the Middelalderparken dealers, but also of Dag making his deliveries. Oh and of you too. And me."

Larsen opened the laptop. It whirred into life. "The screen's broken."

She turned it to him. A great black splodge, like an oil puddle, and just the edges of the photograph of Blackwood outside the Stovner police station.

"It's just the screen that's damaged. The data is still intact. You could pull it all off."

"And how do I say this came into my possession? I tell my boss I'm working with a suspect who has a false passport?"

"What do you mean? My passport is good."

"Your passport is good, yes. It's you that is false."

Blackwood felt a pang of hurt. He didn't know why. He didn't need this cop's approval. "And how do you know that?" he asked.

"I know a liar when I see one."

"That's unfair," he said. "I'm trying to do what's right here."

"What's your name?" she asked. "I know you're not really Owen Blake. So what's your real name?"

Blackwood shook his head.

"So there, you see," she said. "You're all the evidence I have to save my son. And you're a walking lie."

Blackwood took a long sip of his coffee, his mind racing. He took out the photo of Kalle Engelson and his friend, the two dead boys, smiling and making gang signs before a café or bar, just half the sign visible: ...*akkevik*.

He slid it across the table and prodded it. "This place. Where is this?"

Larsen thought about it. "Karakkevik. It's a bar in Bryn."

"Gang owned?"

She shrugged. "Most probably. There are many of them. And those that aren't owned are paying protection money."

"Rune Prestegård wanted these boys scared off, so it's definitely gang rivalry. And he most likely had Dag Engelson shot too, so this is our connection."

"But you said yourself, Prestegård didn't order their killing. It was someone else."

"I know. And they'll know who."

Blackwood tossed a 20 kroner note on the table and marched out to the street. Larsen scrambled in his wake.

23

The Karakkevik bar was a small place on the outskirts of town. The bar seemed quiet, the only activity being a group of burly men sat at a table outside under a canopy, drinking coffee and smoking. There was a heater beside them.

Blackwood and Larsen took them in as they cruised past.

"They don't look like they're here to have a good time," Larsen said.

"No," said Blackwood. He looked back at the bar as it faded into the distance; he could almost feel the menace emanating from it.

His attention snapped back to Larsen's car as something caught his eye in the rearview mirror: another car had pulled out behind them, following them closely down the street.

Blackwood cleared his throat and murmured. "We have company."

Larsen tensed and glanced into her mirror. "You sure?"

"No, but looks familiar," said Blackwood calmly. "Keep driving. Go round the block."

Larsen gripped the wheel tightly and stepped on the gas for a few seconds, putting distance between them and their pursuer before taking the first corner.

The car took the corner behind them.

They drove in silence and Larsen turned again. This time, the pursuer drove on and did not follow.

"They've gone," Larsen said.

"But pretty clear they're tailing us. They'll be back."

They circled the block and parked opposite the bar. The three men were still sat outside and hadn't looked over at all.

"Let's go," Blackwood said, jumping out.

Larsen scrambled out and held his arm. "Wait. We can't just walk in there and interrogate a gang leader."

"Sure you can. Just flash your badge."

"I'm not allowed to use my I.D. anymore. I'm suspended."

"Okay," Blackwood said. "We'll do it my way."

Larsen called after him as he pushed on. "Wait. Please don't do anything to make my suspension permanent."

The three men watched as Blackwood crossed the street and strode towards them. As it became clear he was heading for the bar, one of them rose.

"Vi er stengt," he said.

Blackwood smiled and didn't stop.

The man put his palm out.

In a flash, Blackwood grabbed his hand, twisted. A sickening snap sounded out and the man was on his knees, howling.

The other two men shot up from their chairs, but they were too fat and slow. They rose only to face the barrel of Blackwood's Kahr P9.

"You have a gun?" Larsen cried.

"I borrowed it from Kjetil Bergman."

"My god!"

"Inside," Blackwood said.

The two men scrambled through the door, stepping over their fallen comrade. Blackwood dragged him up and kicked him so he half flew, half scrambled into the bar.

The place was empty. A long bar counter stretched across the room, lined with stools and behind it, a row of taps. It looked like it might be a decent place, if anyone but a gang of criminals ever came to try it out.

"You two, take a seat. Hands on your head."

The two men complied, squirming and seething. The man whose hand he'd snapped pushed himself up into a chair, and Blackwood put the gun to his head. "Now, I reckon you're the leader of this shitty outfit. Am I right?"

"Unlucky for you," the man spat.

"What's your name?"

The man growled defiance. Blackwood dug the Kahr P9's barrel hard into his temple.

"Teo Molund," he said with a half laugh, as if this was all a misunderstanding and could be sorted out over a drink.

"Okay, Teo Molund," Blackwood said. "You're going to talk."

"You're not going to shoot me dead," the man said, smirking.

"You're right. I wouldn't do that. The nice police lady here told me not to kill anyone." Blackwood swiped the pistol away from his forehead and dug it into his crotch. "But I will shoot your balls off. Not both. Just one of them. You can choose which one. Left or right?"

Molund's face turned a sickly green cast, almost verdigris, and he swallowed. "You wouldn't—"

"I took this gun from one of Kjetil Bergman's men a couple of hours ago. Still has his prints on it. I shoot your left testicle off and no one is going to think it's anything but two rival small time bottom feeder crooks having an argument. Now, you choose. Left or right?"

"Okay, okay," the man said. "What do you want to know?"

Blackwood flashed the photograph before him. Molund squinted and moved his head back to focus.

"These two boys. They're yours, yes?"

"What about it?"

"They're dead now."

Blackwood checked Molund's eyes for any hint of surprise, but there was nothing.

"He knows," Larsen said.

"They're dead now, because of you," Blackwood said. "Because of you and your stupid fucking greed."

"Those boys are nothing to do with me. I—"

Molund didn't get to finish his sentence. Blackwood smacked the Kahr P9 across his face.

A couple of teeth clattered across the laminate floor. Molund howled and held his mouth, blood pouring through his fingers.

"You groomed those boys and now someone has shot them dead. Because of you, you piece of shit. Who did it? Who wants you out of business?"

Molund spat through blood and bile. "Kjetil Bergman and his gang. They want to wipe us out."

Larsen, arms folded and watching calmly, said, "We have strong evidence that it wasn't Kjetil Bergman. It was someone else. We want to know who."

"Then you know nothing!"

Blackwood jabbed the gun in his temple again. "Tell us."

"Kjetil Bergman is just the performing monkey for that mafia boss, Rune Prestegård. Ask him."

"I already have. He didn't have those boys shot."

"Then ask him about shooting dead my courier."

Blackwood looked at Larsen. What was this? "Dag Engelson was your courier?"

"They shot him dead. Not me."

"What was he couriering?"

Molund sneered. "Fuck you."

Blackwood jammed the gun into his crotch. "Okay. Left or right? You choose. I'll try my best to get one, but I can't promise I won't blow your cock off."

"The paintings!" Molund squealed. "The fucking paintings!"

Again, Blackwood and Larsen shared a dumbfounded look.

"The Munch paintings?" Larsen asked.

Molund nodded.

"You were smuggling stolen art?"

"Yes!"

Blackwood took the gun away. The two heavies sitting against the wall with their hands on their head shifted in their seats. Blackwood waved the Kahr P9 in their direction and they thought better of it.

"Let's go," Larsen said.

"But we haven't—"

"It doesn't matter. Come on." She marched out of the place.

Blackwood backed out, his gun still pointed at the seething men.

24

Blackwood hurried across the street to Larsen's car, the Kahr P9 thrust deep into his jacket pocket. Hidden, but ready to whip out if Molund and his goons thought of chasing them.

He dived in and Larsen hit the gas. They were a few blocks away in moments. He kept his eye on the rear-view mirrors to see if they were being followed but it seemed safe.

"Why did you leave it there?" he asked. "We don't have any kind of lead."

"What do you think you're doing?" Larsen cried. "You have a gun. Beating up suspects. Violence. I'm a police officer!"

"I thought you were suspended," Blackwood said, cowed by her fury.

"That's not the point! You can't go running around like some fucking... *Rambo.*"

Blackwood stifled a laugh.

"Fuck!" Larsen yelled, exasperated, and tried not to laugh herself. "Give me the gun."

"Uh uh. No way."

"Then promise me you won't use it again."

Blackwood folded his arms. "Do you even know the kind of scum you're dealing with?"

"I spent the entire morning questioning them. I deal with them every fucking day. You have no idea what it's like here. No idea at all."

She drove on and a sullen silence settled between them.

"Anyway, we do have a lead," she said. "The paintings."

"What paintings?"

"A month ago," Larsen explained, "three Edvard Munch landscapes, on loan to a gallery in St Petersburg, were stolen. You don't know about them?"

Blackwood shrugged. "No. Sorry."

"Well, it's a big story here in Norway. The nation is desperate to recover them, and there's a rumour that they are back here. A tip-off about a crooked art dealer who might be fencing them."

"Are you saying Dag Engelson was some international art thief?"

"No. Just a courier."

Blackwood remembered how they'd taken something from the rear of the truck. Not the two tonnes of reindeer meat. Something light. Something they'd simply lifted and put in the boot of their car.

"Why are low level criminals like that," he hooked his thumb back to the road behind them, "dealing in art theft? It seems a bit upmarket for them."

Larsen shook her head. "The lowest criminal gangs deal in stolen art."

"How come?"

"It's big money. It's portable. It's easy to steal. Galleries have million-dollar artefacts on the walls and supermarket security."

"So your average street corner drug dealer is fencing Picassos to the art world?"

"That's about the size of it," Larsen said. "The main problem is they don't care about the art. If it's ever recovered, it's usually damaged."

"Surely that would knock a lot of value off an artwork?"

"Yes, but criminals are deeply stupid people."

She veered left, taking a sharp turn, the tires screeching. A horn sounded behind them and someone shouted.

"Where are we going?" Blackwood asked.

"We're going to see an art dealer."

25

The engine hummed, a low and steady thrum as the car cut through the underpass that snaked under the city centre. Larsen's grip on the steering wheel was firm, assured, her eyes fixed ahead.

"Feels like we've been in this tunnel since yesterday," Blackwood muttered, shifting in his seat to face Larsen. Her profile was all sharp angles against the sporadic tunnel lights.

"Almost there," she said, her voice level, betraying nothing of the adrenaline rush from earlier.

Light at the end, then they were spilling into dimming daylight, snowflakes caught in the glow of the headlights. Dusk wrapped the city in a shroud of grey, the snowfall blurring the lines between sky and land. The city blurred past, skeletal trees reaching for the heavens. He knew this route – they were coursing west, swerving around the heart of the city, and the coroner's office where they'd left Kalle Engelson, cold and still, just hours before.

"Jakob Varg," Larsen broke the silence, "was on my list of suspects to visit today but I didn't get round to him."

"More interested in chasing me." His tone had an edge he hadn't meant.

"Well, of course," she said. "You were my only lead on a murder case."

They both stared ahead, the road unwinding, the case sprawling before them like the infinite net of city streets.

"Are we going to Uranienborg?" Blackwood asked.

Larsen shook her head. "Varg's place is in Borgen."

The car hugged the coastline. To their left, the seafront stretched, all bleak and grey. Yachts clustered in marinas like mourners at a funeral. Larsen took a northward turn and they left the seafront behind, heading into the heart of the city along dual carriageways busy with the pulse of twilight traffic.

Eventually, she turned off onto a road that seemed to breathe a sigh of relief from the urban crush. It was quieter here, the narrow lane lined with picket-fenced townhouses peeking through winter-bare branches. There was a quaintness that belied the darkness of their pursuit.

"Here we are," Larsen declared, easing the car down a sloping road. The cycle lanes ran like parallel scars down the hill. She stopped before a white clapperboard house. Blackwood scanned the scene: no movement, no life beyond the snowflakes' dance.

"Looks deserted," Blackwood observed, stepping out into the cold. He pulled his collar up, the snow kissing his skin with icy lips.

Larsen didn't reply, pushing open the gate that creaked its own protest. They approached, her footsteps confident despite her suspension. She rang the bell; only silence answered.

"Let's check the back," Blackwood suggested, his voice low. He navigated down the slope, past the windowed eyes of the basement level. Dark. Empty.

At the rear door, he tested the handle — unlocked.

"We can't just break in," Larsen started, but Blackwood was already pushing the door open.

"You're suspended, remember?" he said, a half-grin flashing. "Normal rules don't apply."

She exhaled, a mist of resignation in the wintry air, and followed him into the shadows within.

Blackwood's boots thudded on the concrete floor, Larsen just ahead. The basement offered nothing, a hollow space that echoed back their own breaths and footsteps. They ascended a wooden staircase to the house above, each step creaking under their weight. The house held its breath.

And then, chaos — furry streaks of orange darted down, squealing protests filling the void. Blackwood's hand went instinctively to his sidearm before he realized.

Just cats.

A pair of ginger cats. They circled and scattered to the kitchen. Young, scrappy. They were almost kittens.

Larsen clutched at her chest. "Fucking hell," she gasped.

The stink hit them — sharp, invasive. Ammonia and filth. Cat shit and piss. But beneath it, another layer, one that made Blackwood's gut twist. Death. The unmistakable aroma of rotting corpse. He'd smelt it in too many forsaken places.

"Upstairs," he grunted, nodding.

They moved, silent as the snow outside, creeping up the staircase. The scent thickened with each step, clawing at their nostrils, invading their lungs. At the top, Blackwood pushed a bedroom door, muscles tensed for what lay beyond.

The room was dim, shadows clinging to corners. On the bed, propped like a grotesque doll, sat Jakob Varg. One bullet hole, forehead centre — a crimson halo on the headboard.

"Jesus," Larsen whispered, lifting a hand to her mouth. Her eyes were on the corpse's hands — or rather, the bloody stump of his right hand.

"Looks like someone tortured him before they killed him. Clean cuts, no ragged edges."

Larsen glanced around the room, scanning the blood-spattered sheets. Only a pair of secateurs. "Where are they?"

"I think the cats ate them," Blackwood said.

"Damn," Larsen breathed out, eyes still locked on the grim tableau. She swallowed hard, steadying herself, and tramped out and down the stairs.

Blackwood remained, studying the walls. Oil paintings framed in gilded wood, the strokes bold, colours vibrant. His gaze lingered, questioning their origin. Munch's handiwork? He had no idea.

He expected to hear the sound of Larsen puking up, but instead the kitchen clanged below, punctuated by pitiful mews. Tin grinding, metal on metal. Then, a wet plop

— meat hitting bowls, two, maybe three times. Silence followed, save for the sound of eager feeding.

Blackwood descended.

Larsen met him at the foot of the stairs, her face tightened against the scene they'd left above.

"Upstairs," he started, "the paintings... were they those Munchs?"

She shook her head, a quick dismissal, and an aghast expression.

Blackwood shrugged. He had no idea what the Munch paintings looked like.

Together, they searched the ground floor rooms. Paintings adorned every wall, but none held the landscapes they were after. The study revealed more — papers strewn, lists scrawled with names, contacts from far-off places. Old invoices, yellowed with age. A network of European buyers — Italy, Spain, Germany. Russian signatures looped beneath hefty sums.

"Smuggling," Blackwood muttered, piecing together Varg's secret ventures.

"Seems so," Larsen replied, thumbing through the papers with a detective's precision. "And for years."

Larsen's fingers danced through the pages of an appointment diary, worn leather creaking with each turn. Blackwood leaned in, watching as her eyes darted across the scribbled entries, the furrow between her brows deepening. "Three days ago," she murmured, "an appointment with '88' at 7pm."

"Who's '88'?" Blackwood asked, his voice low.

Larsen chewed on her lip, flipping back and forth between the pages. More initials. More '88'. She hesitated, caught on a thought.

Blackwood squinted at the numbers, the pattern clicking into place. "Neo-nazis use *88* as code for *Heil Hitler*," he said, "because H is the eighth letter of the alphabet."

"Damn," Larsen whispered, almost to herself. The edges of her mouth twitched, words forming then retreating as if censoring herself.

She closed the diary with a snap, tucked it into her coat. "We need to leave."

Outside, the cold bit at their cheeks, snowflakes clinging like whispers of secrets untold. Larsen stopped, a statue among the swirling white. "I can't call this in." Her voice wavered. "I'm not even supposed to be here."

"An anonymous tip, then?" Blackwood suggested, his breath clouding before him.

"No." Larsen pulled out her mobile, screen lighting up her determined face. "There's someone else." Rapid Norwegian spilled from her lips, but only the name 'Sogge' was discernible to Blackwood.

Call done, she pocketed the phone and they headed to the car, the engine coming alive with a growl. At the crossroads, Larsen paused, car idling.

Blackwood turned to her, saw the storm of thoughts in her eyes. "What aren't you saying?"

"A lead I didn't want to pursue," she admitted. "It's a long story."

She was already turning, taking them down a sharp left, tires crunching fresh snow as they headed west on a major road.

Whoever this lead was, they lived outside the city.

26

THE CAR CRUISED OUT of the city and the tall buildings gave way to bleak outposts on a sea of snow fields. Hilly, snow-covered mountaintops filled the horizon, only broken by the occasional skeletal tree. The large brown car trundled along the road.

The houses became more spread out and the snow thicker on the ground. As they climbed up further into the hills, they passed a few lonely farms and small settlements but nothing else.

Blackwood looked out of the window at the vast expanse of white that stretched out in front of them. It was beautiful but also intimidating, with a silent menace that seemed to be lurking in its depths. He shivered despite the warmth inside the car and pulled his jacket tighter around him.

Larsen drove on, seemingly unfazed by their surroundings. Blackwood's mind wandered as he tried to make sense of it all. Dag Engelson had been a courier for Teo Molund, carrying stolen old masters that had been fenced by Jakob Varg. And somehow, Kjetil Bergman's gang had intervened to take the paintings for themselves. Perhaps organised by Rune Prestegård. And at the centre of the storm was a frightened boy: Larsen's son.

They had been driving for ten minutes, when Larsen pulled off onto a side road with a sigh of relief and stopped the car outside an old farmhouse.

"We're here," she said.

Blackwood looked around, confused. "Where are we? What are we doing here?"

Larsen smiled, but it was a sad smile. "I'm not sure," she said, her voice low and uncertain. "Someone who might be able to help us."

"Who?" Blackwood asked.

"You'll see. Maybe."

"What does that mean?"

"I don't know if he'll want to help." She paused and looked out of the window at the farmhouse, her face pensive and thoughtful. "But I guess we'll find out soon enough."

Blackwood unbuckled his seatbelt and opened the door. The cold air hit him like a punch in the face and he felt a chill run through his body. He pulled his coat tighter around him as he stepped out of the car, Larsen following closely behind.

They walked up to the farmhouse, their footsteps crunching in the snow. No one appeared to be home. The windows were dark, and the only sound came from a few birds chirping in the distance. The snow had been trampled down around the entrance, and a path of boot prints circled round to the rear of the house, but that was the only sign of life.

Blackwood felt a chill run through him as he looked at the house. It seemed so silent and still, almost like it was waiting for something to happen. He shivered again and turned to Larsen, who appeared similarly uneasy.

"Should we knock?" he asked.

Larsen nodded, taking a deep breath before she stepped forward and knocked on the door three times in quick succession. They waited for what seemed like an eternity.

Blackwood sensed a presence and turned, stiffening.

An old man stood staring, an axe in one hand.

27

BLACKWOOD WENT FOR HIS gun, for just a moment, but then noticed the sled behind the old man, on which was tied a pyramid of logs.

"Hello, Erik," Larsen said.

The old man gazed at them for an age but did not answer. Instead, he continued on past them, took an armful of logs and walked into the house, leaving the door open.

Larsen followed him in.

Blackwood scooped up the remaining logs and followed.

The inside of the farmhouse was surprisingly warm and cozy, despite its exterior. The last embers of a fire glowed in the hearth. It wasn't much, but it was a welcome respite from the cold outside. There was a large table in the centre of the room, on which sat a computer, giving off a blue glow.

One wall was lined with maps, some of Oslo, others of other cities around Europe, photos and news clippings. A case wall. This man was clearly a cop.

The old man looked up from the fire with surprise and pointed to the log pile. Blackwood piled them up with the rest.

Erik jabbered something in Norwegian.

"Our friend is English," Larsen said.

Erik considered Blackwood, looking him up and down with suspicion. "Friend?" he said. "I have friends now?"

"I'm sorry, Erik," Larsen said. "I truly am."

He poked at the fire and set it roaring. Larsen sat on an armchair, perched on the edge, like someone who wasn't sure she was staying.

Erik looked them both up and down again, scoffed, and pointed to another armchair. Blackwood took a seat.

The old man went to a cabinet, took out three shot glasses and laid them on the tiny coffee table. Then he took out a bottle of amber liquid with a navy blue and red label.

"Linie Aquavit," Blackwood said. "I've heard good things about that."

Erik paused, surprised, and nodded. He poured three shots and handed them out before taking a seat.

Blackwood took a sip, barely a whisper, and savoured the taste. Cardamom and oak and a touch of caramel.

Erik let out a humph of approval. "He knows how to savour a good drink, this friend of ours. Doesn't knock it down like a tourist."

"Erik, this is Owen Blake," Larsen said, almost in apology. Not for the intrusion, Blackwood realized, but because she knew it wasn't his real name. "He's helping me with a case."

Erik looked Blackwood up and down all over again, a look that went right through to his soul. What did he see?

Blackwood took a sip of Aquavit, as much to avoid the man's penetrating gaze.

Erik turned his attention to Larsen. "And what about me? Am I helping you with a case?"

"I'd like to think so," Larsen said.

"I'm not a policeman anymore. Or have you forgotten this?"

Larsen waved to the wall of maps and photographs and news clippings. "But I know you are still interested."

"What makes you think I would want to help you?" Erik said.

"My son is involved in this."

Erik flinched and balled his fists. "Is he all right?"

Larsen nodded. "He's safe. I thought you might help for his sake, if not for mine."

Erik shook his head, as if to shake away her words, to unhear them. He brooded in silent fury for a while and then said, "You believed them."

"I didn't know what to believe," Larsen said.

Erik knocked back his Aquavit and sighed in defeat. "I don't blame you. I'd have believed them too. It's the easiest lie in the world to believe. That's why they use it."

"So they wanted you out of the way. Why?"

"I knew they were corrupt."

"Who?"

"Half of the department is in Rune Prestegård's pocket."

"That's hard to believe."

"I think you know it," Erik said. "That's why you're here."

Larsen shook her head and looked at her lap.

"I had the evidence," Erik continued, addressing Blackwood now. "Until they impounded my computer and loaded it with child pornography. This is what they do to anyone to get them out of the way."

So this was what it was all about, Blackwood thought. Erik had been Larsen's co-worker, but he had dug too deep, so they had destroyed him.

"There was an assassination attempt this morning," Larsen said. "On Martin. Three others have been killed."

"The Middelalderparken shooting?" Erik asked. "And the Stovner hit last night?"

Larsen nodded. "They tried to shoot my son too."

Blackwood saw the pain in her eyes, but she kept it together.

Erik let out a heavy sigh and shook his head. He poured himself another shot of Aquavit, and then, almost as an afterthought, filled Blackwood's glass again. Larsen hadn't touched hers. Erik took a sip of his drink and looked at Larsen with determination in his eyes. "What do you need from me?"

Larsen seemed to relax a little. She told him about the investigation, the shootings, her son's arrest, the Karakkevik bar and the surprise regarding the paintings, then the fate of Jakob Varg and the appointment with a mysterious *88*.

Erik nodded thoughtfully as she spoke, taking the occasional sip of Aquavit to steady himself. When she finished speaking, he placed his glass down on the table and said, "The Oslo police are corrupt. To get anything done, you will have to go outside the law. But then, that's why you're here. And with him."

Larsen nodded and even smiled.

Erik stroked his stubbled chin. "The man who tried to shoot your son, it was probably someone from your own department."

"It can't be," Larsen said. "Why?"

"There are two rival gangs here fighting for control. One of them wants respectability. Rune Prestegård isn't just a gangster. He wants power. That's why he's funding Ingrid Borstad's campaign. And the police are right behind it."

Larsen shook her head. "That can't be true."

"You already know it. You came to hear someone else confirm it."

Still she shook her head. Then she knocked back her Aquavit and grimaced. "Who?" she said.

"I suggest you look at the person closest to you. And if you look closely enough, you might also find the man who murdered your—"

"Don't say it," Larsen snapped.

Erik held his hands up in surrender. "It's just, you must know that—"

"I said don't. Please, don't go there. I don't want to hear it."

"Fine," Erik said, with a hint of petulance. A man whom no one listened to. A Cassandra.

Blackwood could see a light of understanding in Larsen's eyes as she realized what Erik was suggesting. She nodded slowly, her face set in determination.

"Thank you," she said. "I will look into it."

28

Blackwood stepped out first and Larsen followed. Snow was falling and the light was fading. Soon it would be night. The icy wind gnawed at his face but the Aquavit still glowed in his chest.

They paused to admire the snow's simple beauty, how it appeared to be floating, like specks of gunpowder in the air.

They walked back to the car, Blackwood keeping an eye out for any further disturbances in case they were being watched or followed. But there was nothing – only the wind howling through the trees, like a warning of danger yet to come.

"Do you believe him?" Blackwood asked.

Larsen thrust her hands into her coat pockets and nodded. "He's lost everything. Men who have nothing to lose rarely lie."

"So what was that other thing? The thing you didn't want to hear?"

Larsen shook her head. "Old history. It's something I don't—"

Before she'd finished her sentence, Blackwood reached out to still her.

A disturbance in the treeline. Someone watching.

A dark figure dashed out, sprinting away.

Blackwood ran on instinct like a ratter.

The figure flashed through the undergrowth as they fled. Difficult to make out. Male. Late thirties. Not fit. Dark overcoat and beanie hat.

Blackwood circled down the path. Up ahead, the figure broke cover and ran for a car.

A blue Volvo parked by the roadside where Larsen had turned off the road earlier.

The man jumped into the car and started it up.

The engine roared and the wheels spun on the gravel as he accelerated away.

Blackwood put on a burst of speed, but it was hopeless. He watched helplessly as the Volvo sped off into the dusk.

The roar of a car behind him made Blackwood scurry to the side of the road. Larsen skidded to a halt beside him and wound down the window.

"Get in!" she shouted above the roar of the engine.

Blackwood jumped into the passenger seat and Larsen gunned it, swerving back onto the road and taking off in pursuit of their mystery man.

"Same car as earlier," Blackwood said.

The Volvo was a few hundred yards ahead of them, weaving in and out of traffic as it sped down the hillside towards Oslo. Larsen kept her foot pressed to the floor, but even she couldn't match its speed. Through fading light and a blizzard of snowfall, they sped after it.

And then, he was no longer on the road ahead.

"Where did he go?" Larsen said.

Blackwood swore under his breath as he craned to see any turn offs where he might have hidden, but there was nothing.

"Who was it?" Larsen asked.

Blackwood shook his head. "Not criminal, or police."

"How do you know?"

"Didn't look the type."

A short man in a black coat and a beanie hat. A lean face, more the studious type than a fighter, and not just because of the glasses he wore. The way he'd scurried away spoke more of fear. Not a man used to handling himself.

Blackwood leaned back in the seat, his mind racing with possibilities. "Could be internal affairs?" he muttered. "Maybe they're following you."

"Could be," Larsen agreed, her knuckles white on the steering wheel.

"When did we first see them?" Blackwood asked, trying to remember.

"Just before we arrived at the Karakkevik bar."

"But I'd seen them before that. Or at least I thought I had."

"So after my interview with Internal Affairs. But if it's them, why run? Why not confront me? I'm a cop they're investigating and I go call on an ex-cop they've already had expelled from the force."

"Maybe he's not Internal Affairs."

"Then what?"

Blackwood shrugged. "I don't know. We need to find out. Can you check the license plate?"

Larsen shook her head, her eyes fixed on the road. "Not now. And besides, there's no one in my department I can trust. You heard what Erik said."

Blackwood nodded, his mind still racing. "So who do we trust then? Who do we turn to?"

Larsen thought for a moment, then she said, "I'm stuck with you."

Blackwood grimaced. If he was the only person she could trust, she wasn't in a good place. He was about to say so when her phone bleeped.

She snatched it up and answered, one hand on the steering wheel. "Sogge?" she said.

Blackwood checked her face, but she shared nothing, just listened.

And then she fired off a stream of rapid Norwegian, questions, he could tell, from the rising intonation, but he got no words. Only one that sounded like *under*.

"Fuck!" she screamed and hung up, placing her phone on the dashboard and tapping through screens, trying to keep one eye on the road.

"What is it?"

"My son. They've released him. He's supposed to be under witness protection. They've let him go."

She snatched the phone up again, a ringing tone blurting in her ear. Someone answered.

Blackwood could hear it was Martin's voice.

They spoke a few brief words before she tossed her phone aside, put her foot on the gas and they sped on towards Oslo.

"What is it?" Blackwood asked.

"Fucking stupid police have released him, thrown him out on the streets. I told them not to!"

"Where is he?"

"I told him to go to Oslo cathedral and wait for me."

She pumped the gas pedal steadily, keeping her foot light. She accelerated out of a turn, where the road cut off into oncoming traffic, and passed a slow convoy of cars trundling toward the city. Horns blared in warning as she swerved in between lanes and left them in her wake.

They roared down the hillside towards Oslo.

29

Blackwood questioned her as much as he could but she was distraught, driving in a blind panic, intent on just one thing: to rescue her son.

He knew the feeling. You would do anything to protect your child. It could turn a woman into a tiger. A man into a killer.

She told him what she could.

Sogge had called to warn her they'd released her son. Someone from Stovner police station had told them to let him go. Sogge didn't know who.

"Do you trust Sogge?"

"Yes," she said. "I don't know. Fuck!"

He had called her to warn her. There was that. He'd also been the one who called her earlier to warn her they were coming to arrest Martin. It seemed unlikely he was one of the ones Erik had warned her about.

The sky turned black as they reached the city. Streetlights and neon signs blinked to life as they wound their way through the streets, heading towards Oslo cathedral.

Larsen's grip on the steering wheel was like iron, her face a mask of determination. The streets grew more crowded and Larsen had to slow down, weaving in and out of traffic.

Blackwood checked the mirrors for any sign of pursuit or danger.

When they could drive no further, she parked the car and ran out. Blackwood followed, checking his surroundings. They were a few streets away from his hotel. Despite the cold and the snow falling, the air felt heavy, like a storm was coming. A chill ran through him as he searched for any sign of trouble but saw nothing except the blur of human traffic. He couldn't shake the feeling that something was wrong. A sixth sense he'd always had for imminent trouble.

They dashed across a market square on cobbled streets, edging around a passing tram. And then they were running through an arcade that edged the cathedral, along seated café dwellers.

They reached the entrance of the cathedral and Larsen rushed inside. Blackwood followed her, his skin prickling with a sense of danger.

Inside, the cathedral was small, not vast as he'd expected. The ceiling stretched high above him, and he stepped into a wide aisle on polished stone. Thin streams of light from coloured windows illuminated frescoes that he barely noted. He saw a blaze of gold over the lamps and candles burning; reds, blues and greens shimmered over the columns that held up the arches framing the altar, decorated in white and gold like a wedding cake. That stifling echo of cloistered meditation that had always made him uneasy. Like some god was shushing him in the great library of life.

Larsen ran up the central aisle, checking the pews. A handful of tourists and worshippers milled all around.

"Martin?" Larsen called.

People looked around and glared at the disturbance.

Blackwood had scanned every seat and every person and knew the boy wasn't there.

Behind the altar, he spied a side door ajar. Something not right about it. He strode up the red carpeted steps, skirted the altar and ran through to the vestry.

Footsteps echoed on marble. Two people. Running.

Blackwood pushed through the vestry and came out to a corridor just as a figure disappeared through a rear exit door.

Not enough to identify. Just someone running.

He darted to the heavy wooden door and plunged out to a cobbled street.

Larsen called behind. "Blake!"

Through the general mill of human traffic, the criss-cross of pedestrians, Blackwood focused on two figures fleeing. For an instant he caught them before they disappeared down a side street.

One older man dragging a teenager. Martin.

Weaving between the criss-cross of pedestrians, Blackwood ran to the corner, aware of Larsen sprinting on his heels.

He came out to a dark back street. The boy was being bundled into a car. The abductor glanced back.

Blackwood raised the Kahr P9 and took aim.

The man jumped into the car.

Larsen skidded to Blackwood's side and shouted. "Don't! My son is in that car!"

She was right. It was too dangerous.

Blackwood shoved the gun back into his belt and ran.

The car roared away.

It was hopeless. He gave up.

Larsen joined him, shrieking, "He's gone! They have my son!"

Blackwood watched the car skid and turn far up the road and disappear. "It was your partner," he said. "It was Sogge. I think."

"Sogge?" she cried. "But then it can't be Haaken."

"Who?"

Sirens wailed, growing louder. Blackwood realized they had been approaching for the past minute or more.

Larsen jabbed at her phone. "No answer," she said. "From either of them."

"I think those sirens are for us," Blackwood said.

At the far end of the back street, an unmarked car roared into view. A police car, lights flashing, came right behind it.

"Spesialenheten," Larsen said.

"What's that?"

"Internal Affairs." She turned to Blackwood, gripped his lapels, and hissed, "Get my son! I don't care how you do it. Just get him back."

Blackwood nodded and checked the Kahr P9 at the small of his back. A cold, uncomfortable presence. He would need it.

He slipped away round the corner and walked swiftly through the throng of pedestrians in the market square.

Before the cars had screeched to a halt at Detective Sergeant Larsen's feet, he stepped onto a tram and the doors closed behind him.

30

Blackwood leaned against the tram's metal pole, his mind racing. He needed a plan, but for the first time, he felt adrift. Detective Sergeant Larsen's son was taken, perhaps by the very man who'd tried to shoot him dead this morning. And Blackwood had no way of finding out where he was.

Had it been Sogge? The man had been tall and wide with a fur hat. He wore a black puffa jacket that could have been police issue — it was difficult to tell in the blur of snow.

It had been dark and they had always been some distance ahead, but the man matched Sogge's build and gait, and that something else, something indefinable: the essence of a person. He would stake his life on it.

It was Sogge.

How could he track him? He recited the car's registration number over and over in his mind. Who could trace it?

Perhaps Erik.

Blackwood could steal a car, hotwire it and drive back to the old man. Erik could probably trace the owner of the car. But that wouldn't tell him where it was.

Perhaps Erik had photos of surveillance. Locations the corrupt police might be using.

Surveillance photos. Like those on Prestegård's laptop.

Larsen's car. She'd parked the car and jumped out in the mad rush to the cathedral. He tried to remember if she'd left the keys in the ignition, but it was all lost in the haze of panic. She had definitely left Prestegård's laptop. He thought back. She had shoved it under her seat, out of sight.

The tram trundled through Oslo streets and Blackwood peered through the gloom, matching the terrain to the map in his mind. The tram slowed. They were approaching a stop. Taking one last glance out of the window at the darkening sky, Blackwood jumped off and circled back towards the cathedral.

He hurried through the narrow streets, his eyes scanning the area for any signs of danger. As he approached the spot where Larsen had parked the car, he saw that it was still there.

And that someone was opening the door. A man in a black coat and beanie hat. The man who had been tailing them all afternoon.

Blackwood trudged on calmly, head down, as unobtrusive as possible, till he was right next to him, and then he pounced.

The man was peering into the car, uncertain if he should get in. He yelped in surprise as Blackwood grabbed him by the collar and slammed him against the side of the car.

"What are you doing here?" Blackwood demanded.

The man stammered something unintelligible and tried to squirm out of Blackwood's grip, but he couldn't break free.

"Who sent you?" Blackwood asked.

The man shook his head, still struggling to get away, but Blackwood held him tight. He was weak. No fighter. What Blackwood had noticed in an instant of seeing the man flee, he could now feel. Not a criminal, nor a cop. This man had never been in a fight in his life.

"Don't hurt me," he said, switching to English. "I know you're an assassin."

"What?" Blackwood said. He tightened his grip. This was the moment where an assailant could take you by surprise. Say something to put you off guard and then strike.

But the man did nothing, just squirmed and adjusted his glasses.

"You're an assassin working with the police. You can't do anything here. I'll shout out. People will notice."

A police siren wailed in the distance as if to underscore his threat.

"Why would you think that?" Blackwood asked.

"It's clear you have a military background, Mister Blake. And you're tracking down gang members in Oslo. I know all about you and have all the information on my work computer ready to be released if you kill me."

He was almost in tears now.

Blackwood loosened his grip and pulled out the Kahr P9.

The man whimpered.

"Get in the car."

The man clambered into the driver's seat while Blackwood opened the rear door and sat right behind him.

"If you try to jump out, I'll shoot you."

"Please, don't."

"Hands on the steering wheel. Who are you?"

"Kalland," the man stuttered. "Anders Kalland. I'm a reporter for Dagbladet, it's one of Oslo's newspapers."

"I know what it is," Blackwood said. While he couldn't read Norwegian, he'd noticed the racks of newspapers and noted the titles.

Now it made sense. A journalist, tailing a cop and what appeared to be a foreign agent.

"I'm going to reach into my pocket for my card," Kalland said. His trembling hand came out with a business card and Blackwood snatched it and read it. It was, sure enough, a business card for a journalist with Dagbladet. Blackwood pocketed it.

"How do you know my name?"

Kalland scoffed, confident for the first time. "I'm a j—"

"Journalist, yes. I know."

"And it's obvious Owen Blake is a false identity."

"Why do you think I'm an assassin working for the police?"

"You were involved in the shooting at Stovner last night but released this morning. Only to be involved in another gang shooting this morning. It's very clear you have a military background, Mister Blake. And you're tracking down gang members in Oslo."

Blackwood silently shifted the gun to point at the footwell and pondered this. "Why do you think the police are involved?"

"I've been getting information from an anonymous source within the police department. There are off-the-books assassinations taking place. A shoot to kill policy."

Blackwood wondered if this anonymous source was Erik. Did Kalland know that Erik might be his source, or was he just some corrupt ex-cop to him? Ironically, Erik was saying the exact same thing.

"If you shoot me here," Kalland said, "I have a great deal of evidence that points to you and Detective Sergeant Kari Larsen of the Stovner police department. If you sh—"

"I'm not going to shoot you. I'm not an assassin. I'm just a traveller passing through who's got involved in all of this. You're right, though. I am ex-military. I'm looking for a missing teenager. Larsen's son. I'm helping her with that. But you can't say anything about that."

"As I thought."

"What is it you think? What do you think is going on?"

"Larsen's son is involved with the gangs."

"That's true. And she's trying to extract him. She's trying to save him. Someone tried to shoot him at the incident this morning. That someone might now have kidnapped him again. I'm trying to rescue him."

Kalland pondered this, his eyes on Blackwood in the rear-view mirror.

"That's why I've been taking a tour of every gang member in Oslo today," Blackwood added.

"And every disgraced corrupt cop?"

"I think that man might have more in common with you than you think."

And there it was, the doubt in Kalland's eyes. This reporter didn't know it all and now could see he didn't have the entire picture.

"How much surveillance do you have on this story?" Blackwood asked. "Do you know where a corrupt cop might have taken this boy?"

"I might, yes," Kalland said.

"Reach under your seat. There's a laptop."

Kalland leaned forward with a huff and pulled out the damaged laptop.

"That belongs to Rune Prestegård. The screen is broken but I'm sure you'll be able to access the data. In exchange, you're going to give me a lead. A boy's life is at stake and we have very little time."

"Okay," Kalland said. "I'm going to reach into my bag now."

He pulled out a tablet and opened it, holding it high for Blackwood to see. He swiped through a series of photos. It was so similar to Rune Prestegård's collection of surveillance photos that Blackwood thought he was looking at the same information. But no, these were different places.

Various criminal types gathering at locations around the city: a scrapyard, an industrial estate, a run-down hotel.

None of the men in the photographs were Sogge, but Blackwood recognized a couple of Kjetil Bergman's guys and one of Prestegård's men.

Blackwood studied the photos intently, his eyes darting from one to the other. He was looking for something, some clue that might tell him which of these places was linked to Martin's disappearance.

Finally, Blackwood stopped at one of the photos and pointed at it. "That one. Let me look closer at that guy."

Kalland pinched a close-up of a figure standing at a corrugated fence. There was no doubt about it. It was Sogge.

"Where was this taken?"

"This one is taken at the scrapyard in Tveita. It's a typical money laundering front."

Blackwood took a few photos of the tablet. "Okay. You can get out now."

Kalland paused, dumbfounded. "What?"

"Take the laptop. Find out what's on it. If it's anything useful, call me. No one else."

Kalland shoved the laptop into his satchel, zipped it up and got out of the car. He didn't look back as he scurried away, disappearing into the night.

Blackwood turned his attention back to his phone. He swiped through the photos one last time, then got in the driver's seat and punched the ignition.

31

Larsen knew this was serious, because her very own Internal Affairs investigators took her to Oslo central station, not Stovner.

The imposing glass-fronted building swallowed them whole and they parked in the cavernous underground car park. She tried to remember their names. It was only an hour or two ago but a lifetime since.

Olav Volden and Maria Westrum. That was it.

This morning had been a query, a warning, a shot across the bows. But now it was an official investigation by the Norwegian Bureau for the Investigation of Police Affairs.

As they bustled her into an interrogation room, she caught sight of her boss, Henrik Haaken, talking with Superintendent Kjell Thorstad. That was how serious it was.

Detective Chief Inspector Haaken glanced over with a look of bewilderment. With the look of a supervisor who didn't like being hauled in to account to his boss. A look of *what the hell have you done?*

She searched his face for signs of guilt. Henrik Haaken. *HH. 88.* That was what Jakob Varg's diary had suggested. But now Sogge was the guilty one. Could Sogge be *88?* Or could they both be working together?

Superintendent Kjell Thorstad, the big police chief she only ever saw on TV, towered over Haaken with a look of thunder. He was tall and thin, with a strong jaw and a stern expression. He wore a crisp grey suit and a white shirt, with a black tie. His grey hair was combed back neatly. He commanded the room with a presence that demanded respect.

In the interrogation room, it was just Westrum and Volden, but Haaken and Kjell Thorstad would be behind the mirror, watching it all.

"I want it on record immediately," Larsen spat, "that my son has been kidnapped and is in great danger. We are wasting time."

"Detective Sergeant Kari Larsen," Volden began. "We are here to formally charge you with—"

"Listen to me! My son is kidnapped. I am trying to find him. The stupid police here, in this building, let him go."

Maria Westrum leaned forward, lowering her voice in what she imagined to be soothing. "Detective Sergeant Larsen. This morning you were taken off the case. You are suspended. You promised you would go home and have nothing to do with police matters. We have you on record as saying that. And yet you have continued in your investigation."

"I am trying to protect my son."

Volden swiped through a tablet. "After being suspended this morning, you visited a former associate. One given a dishonourable discharge. Why would you do that?"

"I can visit an old colleague if I like," Larsen said.

"One guilty of possessing child pornography?"

Larsen said nothing in response, simply shrugged.

Maria Westrum shook her head, sad, disappointed.

Larsen felt a ball of rage lodge in her throat. "While we're on the subject of child protection, perhaps you can tell me why this station released my child from witness protection and threw him out onto the streets, where he is at the mercy of the criminal gang who groomed him?"

"That is not what we're here to—" Volden began.

"And who, as a result of such incompetence, has now been kidnapped by that criminal gang." She slammed her fist on the desk and a froth of spittle landed on the table.

Maria Westrum couldn't stop herself from jerking back in her seat.

Volden continued. "You also visited one Karakkevik bar, a known hangout for one of the city's criminal gangs. The owner of the bar was threatened by you and the Irish national, Owen Blake."

Larsen flinched.

How could they know about that? A gangland boss like Teo Molund would surely never report anything like that to the police.

Volden angled the tablet to show a grainy CCTV photo. A man photographed from above, standing at a shop counter.

"This man, Owen Blake, who is a criminal suspect—"

"He is innocent of any crime," Larsen said.

"He is a shadowy figure, a possible criminal or foreign agent. We strongly suspect he is linked to a border incident and a recent spate of killings in the north. Dag Engelson ferried him from Tromsø. We have this CCTV footage of him buying a burner phone on the day Engelson set out from there. Police there want him to help with their enquiries into a crime gang turf war in the Finnmark."

Larsen viewed the grainy photo.

It was Owen Blake.

There was no doubt about it. There was something in the impersonal sheen of a blurry CCTV still that implied guilt, that suggested a crime, because this was the medium of the dark hearted murderer: the grainy, washed-out portrait of a monster walking among us.

Larsen slumped in her seat, the bitter bile of defeat and betrayal seeping through her.

32

Blackwood noted the further east he drove, the shabbier Oslo became, till he was cruising along a tired strip of T-shirt shops and kebab houses. The tall lights on the sheet-metal signs flickered and blinked. Some businesses were actual storefronts; others were just tarp stretched between tree stumps and other makeshift structures. Oslo wasn't so much a city as a collection of unconnected outposts.

He drove on past the scrapyard and checked for signs of life. The gate was locked and a tired wooden fence blocked off everything but the mountains of scrap cars. Somewhere inside the compound a light shone for a moment and then was gone.

He circled the block and noted two entry points at the back where he might fit through: under an old brick arch and through a gap in a chain link fence. The rest of the area was a wire jungle, packed with rusting metal walls, piled cars, and junked machinery.

Finally, he parked Larsen's car on a side street that was only used by delivery trucks and employees with their own parking stickers.

He pulled up the satellite view on Google Maps and panned over to the construction site. It was an old satellite photo, he knew, but it gave him a rough idea of the layout: the paths between the piles of cars, and the two or three outbuildings. All of those were unchanging. But still, the map was never the terrain.

Blackwood stepped out of the car and looked around. The street was quiet, but he could hear a distant hum. He slipped into the shadows and made his way around the back of the scrapyard, keeping an eye out for security cameras or any other signs of life. He reached the gap in the fence he had seen earlier and paused to assess it.

Reaching out, he grasped the wire mesh with both hands and tested its strength. It felt solid but, as he pulled and twisted, it gave way. Soon enough, he'd made a gap large enough to squeeze through. On the other side, he crouched low and surveyed the scene.

The satellite image did not give an indication of the sheer scale of it. Thousands of vehicles had been dumped there, clustered in great hills like iron filings around magnets. Great metal birds who bled gas and oil when grounded by gravity. Even in the night he could see the cars were dusty and dented from where they had been wedged into place by boot heels after being offloaded from the lorries.

He crept on through the compound, making sure to stay in the shadows, keeping an eye out for any patrols or guards. His heart thumped in his chest as he drew closer to the outbuilding, but luckily there was no one around and no dogs barked.

As he crept closer, the hum of activity got louder. He recognized it now as the sound of men talking in one of the outbuildings. He paused and listened intently, trying to make out what they were saying. It sounded like an argument, but he couldn't make out any words.

He inched around the larger of the prefabricated huts.

Bright light glared from a window. Perhaps the flash of light he'd seen as he drove past.

He peered inside. Just for a single second and slid back under cover.

A group of men sitting around a table playing cards. Six in all. Another man sitting away from them closer to the door, entranced by his phone.

Several weapons on display. One Glock on the table. The handle of another poking out from under a jacket. And a Kalashnikov sat across the lap of the man guarding the door.

There would be more. Every man in the hut would be carrying. It was that kind of gathering.

Blackwood sidled along the building, ducking under the window. He made his way deeper into the compound and skirted a smaller hut.

A dimmer light shone from inside, a pale blue light that flickered. The unmistakable ambience of a television.

He peeped inside to survey the interior. Again, just a second was enough.

Two sentries, both armed but docile. One nodding off in his chair, the other staring out the television like it was an uninvited guest. Two other figures in the room. The sullen hulk of Sogge, slumped in a chair and dozing.

And Martin, sitting up on a mattress against the wall, hugging his knees, his eyes on the television but not watching.

Blackwood crept along the side of the prefab till he came to the door. He held his breath and scanned the scene.

There was nothing in the rest of the compound. No one to see what would happen next.

He turned the Kahr P9 around so he was gripping the barrel, took a deep breath, and kicked the door open.

The sentry who was awake got the gun butt full in the face. His nose split open, he choked, snapped his head back, and crumpled.

The second woke, startled, and made to leap up, blinking, reaching inside his jacket.

Blackwood elbowed him between the eyes. With a sickening crack, he fell, unconscious.

Sogge was already on his feet and barrelling for him like a great bear.

Blackwood's boot smashed him between his legs. He doubled over and his face met Blackwood's knee. His head snapped up for just a moment before he fell like a bag of bricks.

"Come on, Martin. Quick."

The boy sprang up and, in a moment, they were outside, running along the rear of the huts, their boots pounding ice and frozen mud.

Too much noise. They should have crept out. Too late.

He careened on through the darkness, the boy right beside him.

The voices behind came too soon. Then the gunshot.

A single shot pinged off metal, sending a spark flying above Martin's head.

He pushed the boy in front and fired off a blind round behind. No aim. Just enough to scare them.

Shouts and cries filled the air.

"Over there!" he cried.

Martin ran for the fence and scurried through the gap.

Bullets zinged off the fence all around them like firecrackers.

Blackwood turned and fired off two shots.

One of the men screamed and fell.

Blackwood squeezed through, the chicken wire snagging his jacket. It tore as he pulled away.

They jumped out of sight just as machine gun fire strafed the fence.

The rest was a desperate sprint for the parked car. They dived inside and before he could hit the gas, more shots zipped by them, one taking off the wing mirror.

"Get down!" he yelled, pushing Martin so he was almost crouched in the footwell.

He gunned the car out of there, but before he could turn out of the street, their cars came roaring out of the compound.

33

Larsen swallowed and shook her head. "I'm not convinced that is him."

It was him. She knew it. But this man they described. Whatever had happened in the north, she had seen the essential goodness in the man. This had never failed her. In twenty years of policing. Not once.

"And anyway," Larsen continued, rising from her seat. "That man has only helped me to locate my son, whom you have put in danger. Now. You have wasted enough of my time with your incompetence. I need to find my son."

Maria Westrum patted the air between them and gave the face of a concerned mother. "Detective Sergeant Larsen, we cannot allow you to—"

The door opened and Haaken strode in, barring her way for a moment. Superintendent Kjell Thorstad slipped into the room behind him but said nothing.

"Wait for me out there," Haaken said. "Just a moment."

Larsen marched out of that claustrophobic room and breathed a little deeper. Haaken closed the door, against which their muffled shouts pounded.

She paced the stub of corridor that opened out to the vast open plan office where city colleagues worked at desks. So much paperwork in this city and so little work out there on the streets.

That man in the photo. The man who called himself Owen Blake. A spate of killings and a border incident, Westrum had said. What was he? Had she allowed herself to trust a man who was nothing but a killer, a mercenary?

She had to get out of here. She had to go save her son.

She was about to storm out of the place when Haaken burst out of the interrogation room, took her elbow and marched her towards the exit. She craned her neck back to see Westrum and Volden arguing with Kjell Thorstad, who patted the air between them as if to dampen their ardour.

"Look, Larsen," Haaken said. "This is a shit show. They want you arrested. They want you locked up so you can't interfere anymore."

"This is ridiculous," Larsen protested. "My son is kidnapped."

They halted, twenty yards from the exit and freedom. She glanced back at Kjell Thorstad again. He stormed off, leaving Maria Westrum red faced with impotent rage.

"I spoke for you," Haaken said. "I assured Thorstad you were clean and you would no longer interfere. That's the price for you not being in cuffs right now."

Larsen folded her arms across the aching emptiness in her womb. "Well, thanks, I suppose."

Superintendent Kjell Thorstad strode out of the police station and passed them without giving them a glance; a busy politician with places to go, a city to run. But for a brief part of his day, he'd come here, to see her, a lowly detective from Stovner, being questioned. That had been important. Whatever it was she and her son and Owen Blake were involved in, it concerned men like Kjell Thorstad.

"But you have to tell me what the hell is going on," Haaken said.

Again, she searched his face for signs of guilt, corruption, something that would make it clear he was behind all of this. But there was nothing. Haaken looked as bewildered and befuddled as he always did.

No. It was Sogge. It must be.

"There are colleagues on the inside," Larsen whispered. "They are in the pay of the criminal gangs, working for Rune Prestegård. And I know who it is."

"Tell me," Haaken said.

Larsen hesitated for a moment, her mind racing with the possibilities of what might happen if she revealed the name. But her son's life was at stake. Haaken was the only ally she had left in the department.

"It's Sogge," she said finally, her voice barely above a whisper.

Haaken's eyes widened in surprise. "Sogge? That's impossible. He's a solid officer. Nothing remarkable, but absolutely dependable."

"I know," Larsen said. "But I saw him. He kidnapped my son, and they have him now."

Haaken stroked his stubbled chin. "Okay, I will handle this."

"We have to find him now. My son."

"I'll call Sogge in. But leave it with me. You can't get involved. I will sort this out."

Larsen nodded, a wave of relief sweeping through her heart. Someone believed her. Someone was listening. That was a start.

Haaken ushered her out of the door to the cold night. "Now go home, before Thorstad changes his mind and decides to keep you here. I'll call you as soon as I have your son."

He turned back into the building, already on his phone.

Larsen walked swiftly away, down the slope towards the streetlights. They were running out of time. She couldn't sit around and wait for Haaken to rescue her son. She was a cop. She could handle this.

34

Bullets pinged off the car as they flew away.

Blackwood jacked the accelerator and sped through narrow streets to the city. In the rear-view mirror a fleet of black cars, four, maybe six, buzzed and jostled for position.

He reached out and found Martin's mop of hair. "Are you okay?"

The boy stammered a "yes," and whimpered.

"Stay down," Blackwood yelled.

He jackknifed the car into a squealing turn and came out to a crowded street, neon-lit and buzzing with nightlife. Revellers screamed and scattered.

The black cars pursuing came roaring round the corner.

A siren wailed.

A police car.

He glanced back to see the headlights of his pursuers gaining ground. The blue flashing light leading the others. Cops and criminals pursuing.

He made a sharp right turn onto a deserted street and pushed the car even faster. The engine groaned in protest, but he kept going.

Another siren wailed.

More police.

The black cars of the criminal gang were hanging back now.

This would only end one way: the city's police converging on him. Weapons drawn. A shoot out. A criminal taken down. Case closed.

Blackwood checked his mental map with the terrain. They were driving west back to the heart of the city.

The top of the Cathedral peeked out to the north and flashed past.

He took a series of sharp turns down narrow streets, heading southwest, weaving in and out of traffic and narrowly avoiding collisions with other cars.

The adrenaline pumped through his veins as he raced through the city.

He took a sharp turn down a cobblestone road and swerved around an oncoming truck.

He dodged between two parked cars and then quickly turned again into a narrow alleyway that led away from the main road.

Blackwood floored the gas and sped down the alleyway, the police cars still in hot pursuit.

He took a sharp turn onto a cobblestone road and the car bounced and shuddered as it struck the rough surface.

The police were gaining on them now, their headlights glaring in the darkness.

Blackwood took a hard left turn onto a side street and then another hard right turn onto yet another side street.

The police cars skidded around the corners trying to keep up with him, but Blackwood was too quick for them.

He veered sharply south and cruised down a stretch of tramline, roaring past an oncoming tram. Its warning bell clanged. Startled passengers peered out of the windows.

The cars followed, undeterred.

There was nothing for it.

Blackwood screeched through a *Road Closed* sign and screamed along a wide pedestrian boulevard, his fist on the horn.

People scattered.

Down a narrow alley, the car burst out onto a small courtyard dominated by a fountain.

He edged around it and skidded down a turn off.

The police cars were right behind them, their sirens blaring. All that was ahead was a set of stairs down to a plaza.

Blackwood took a deep breath and floored the gas pedal.

With a burst of speed, he launched the car off the stairs.

For a moment, time stood still as the car flew through the air.

Martin screamed beside him.

Blackwood focused solely on the road ahead, waiting for the moment of impact.

The car hit the ground with a bone-jarring thud and Blackwood struggled to keep it under control as it sped on, tires screeching against the pavement.

They turned, careening, till the tires gripped asphalt again and he sped off across the plaza.

The police cars pulled up against the steps and skidded to a halt. One tried to follow but bumped down and crashed nose first at the foot of the steps.

Blackwood and Martin snorted relief as they drove away into the night, leaving the police and their pursuers behind.

Pedestrians rushed out of the way, shouting abuse.

In a few moments, they cruised back onto road and Blackwood took a sharp turn onto another street, leaving the chaos behind. He could hear their sirens growing fainter in the distance.

He glanced over at Martin, who was pale and shaking in the passenger seat. "You okay?"

Martin nodded, still too shocked to speak.

Blackwood took a deep breath and focused on the road ahead, knowing they were not out of danger yet. He skidded to a halt down a quiet side street by the side of the entrance to an underground car park.

"Come on. Get out!" he barked.

In moments, he and Martin were striding down the street: two pedestrians out for a hurried evening stroll. Sirens wailed a few blocks away. They passed graffitied walls and a row of hire bicycles. He considered them for a moment, but pushed on, scanning the place for an escape route.

A small car park sat to the side on the end of a block. A free car park with no barrier or ticketing system. Perfect.

He took Martin's elbow and guided him inside, marching towards a black Volkswagen. In a few moments, they were inside and he had hotwired it. They sailed out of there at an easy pace and he cruised westwards away from the blare of sirens.

35

Blackwood drove aimlessly through the dark Oslo streets, past dimly lit buildings and empty sidewalks. Martin was silent, his breathing slow and measured. Blackwood could tell he was still in shock, but he also knew that Martin was tough. He had proven that much tonight.

He turned this way and that, circling back on himself but drifting in a general westerly direction. He wondered if he should cut back and go east, but that made no sense. East was where the chase had started. It made sense to put as much distance between him and his pursuers as possible. However, that was what they would expect. His M.O. had been to always do the opposite. But not now. Not with Martin in the car. He had to get him as far away from danger as possible.

And who was chasing them? There was the question. A criminal gang and the police, both seemingly in it together.

Both, in their different ways, owned these streets. Nowhere was safe.

"Where are we going?" Martin asked.

Blackwood snapped to. "I don't know. We need somewhere safe."

"We could go home."

Blackwood shook his head. "Not safe."

He wondered for a moment if they should go to his hotel room, but no. Sogge himself had taken him to the hotel this morning. The corrupt cop, neck deep in conspiracy. He could never go to that hotel again. His holdall was there, with nothing but a change of clothes and a wad of Euros. A thousand. Less the two hundred he'd pocketed. That eight hundred was almost worth risking death. Eight hundred euros could go a long way for a man as ascetic as Blackwood.

He was thinking of calling Larsen when his phone bleeped.

"Hello?" he said.

Larsen's voice came through, almost a whisper. "Owen. It's me."

"I've got Martin."

She shrieked. A mother's desperate relief. "Thank you. I need you to take him somewhere safe."

Where the hell in this city was safe for this boy, from the police and the criminal gang who were working with them?

"Where do you suggest?" Blackwood asked.

There was a long pause with only Larsen's breathing. She was walking somewhere, trudging through snow.

"Take him to where he can get a good glass of Linie Aquavit."

Blackwood thought about it and said, "Okay."

Larsen hung up and Blackwood let the burner phone fall on his lap. He jerked the steering wheel and took a sharp left.

"Are we going to my mother?" Martin asked.

"Not yet."

Blackwood revved the car up as he took the steep road back up the mountain. It was different in the dark, without seeing the landmarks of remote buildings and the vast, white fields he'd noted this afternoon.

"Tell me about Erik," Blackwood said.

"Erik?"

"An ex-colleague of your mother's."

"Uncle Erik," Martin said, brightening. "Is that where we're going?"

"How well do you know him?"

Martin took a breath, pursed his lips and continued with difficulty. "It wasn't true. What they said about him. All those things."

"How do you know?"

"I know him. All right? He would never do that."

Blackwood mulled this over as he drove on. "So, you feel safe with him?"

"Totally."

"When was the last time you saw him?"

"It was before it all happened. Erik was good to us. He looked after my mother when, you know..."

"After your father died?"

Martin nodded.

"Your father was a cop too?"

"Yeah."

Blackwood nodded, understanding the pain of losing someone close in the line of duty. He had seen it happen too many times.

They drove in silence for a while. The snow was coming down harder now, the flakes hitting the windshield and melting instantly.

Finally, he turned the car onto the narrow road that came to Erik's cabin, nestled in the woods. It was dark, but

Blackwood could see the lights on inside. He parked the car and turned to Martin.

"This is where your mother said I should take you. Are you okay with it?"

Martin snorted a teenager's exasperation and climbed out of the car. That was his eloquent answer.

Blackwood followed him. Erik opened the door and rushed out to greet them, grinning broadly. Larsen must have called ahead to warn him.

Martin fell into his embrace, till Erik held him at arms' length and said, "Look how you've grown."

They bustled inside and Blackwood followed, casting a wary glance outside, checking all was safe.

Erik's cabin was warm and cozy, the same fire crackling in the hearth but now the smell of baked bread wafting through the air. Blackwood took off his jacket, feeling the warmth of the fire embrace him. Erik and Martin were already chatting, catching up on old times.

Blackwood cleared his throat. "Erik, I need to talk to you."

Erik looked at him, his expression turning serious. "What's happened?"

Blackwood explained the situation, about how Martin had been kidnapped, and how the police and a criminal gang were involved. Erik listened intently, his face hardening as Blackwood relayed the story of the last hour or so.

"Well," Erik said, "it's all as I suspected. Rune Prestegård's gang are a mafia and there are elements in the police force who are members."

"I don't think Sogge was with the gang," Martin said.

Blackwood and Erik both looked at him, astonished.

"They kidnapped us both."

"But Sogge was the one who took you," Blackwood said.

"I know, but he said he was keeping me safe. And then we were jumped by the gang. They held us both."

Blackwood's mind raced. Could that be true? Sogge had bundled Martin away in a car. He had only seen Blackwood, not Larsen, fleeing from the cathedral. Could he have seen Larsen chasing? Was he really only trying to protect the boy from Blackwood, this dangerous suspect who might be involved with the gang?

"No," Blackwood said. "It's a classic ruse to get you onside. He pretends to be on your side. Leads you to the gang. They pretend he's a captive too, so he can get the info out of you. Did you talk to him? Did you tell him what was happening?"

Martin looked at his boots. "Yes. A little."

"What did you tell him?"

"That my mother suspected you at first, but then believed you and let you go so you could work for her."

Blackwood sighed. "Shit."

"What?" Martin protested.

"There was a chance, a small chance, that they believed your mother was just a cop trying to get to the bottom of some shootings. Now they know she has me onside and—"

"And nothing," Erik said. "They know what you are and they know what Larsen is: a cop who can't be bought. There's nothing Martin said that can change any of that."

Blackwood looked from Erik to Martin and nodded. "Okay. Fair enough. They're not stupid. You're right."

"So, either Sogge has been left to the mercy of Teo Molund's gang," Erik said. "In which case he's probably dead by now. Or he's still at large and looking for you."

36

Sogge knew he had to get away as quickly as possible. He tore through the woods, leaping over logs, ducking under branches, and fighting through brambles and thickets. His lungs burned with pain but he didn't slow down because if they caught him, it would be all over.

The sun had set and the forest was black. He ran on till he was too exhausted to go any further, halted in a clearing and collapsed. He looked up at the stars twinkling in the night sky and took a deep breath of cool air to steady his pounding heart.

His left arm burned like hell. A bullet had caught him, took a bite out of his sleeve and a chunk of flesh. It stung like acid.

A twig snapped.

A rustle of leaves.

He shot up. Through the murk of the wood, two shadowy figures edging towards him. The gang had followed him into the forest. Heart racing, he scrambled to his feet and sprinted away, weaving through trees and bushes as fast as he could.

He ran for what seemed like hours until he finally stumbled out of the woods onto what seemed like a deserted industrial estate, or an old farm. An outcrop of dilapidated barns. In the distance, torch lights approached from the direction of the woods, but no one was there yet.

He darted towards the row of outbuildings, hoping to find a place to hide. The first door he tried was locked. He moved onto the next one and tried the handle. It turned and he pushed the door open, slipping inside just as the torch lights broke out of the wood.

He eased the door shut and listened for any sounds from outside. Shouting and cursing as they searched for him. He had to stay hidden until they gave up and left the area.

A wooden staircase led up to a second floor. These were certainly some kind of living quarters, maybe for farm labourers. He crept up the stairs, his heart racing with every creak of the old wooden steps. As he reached the top, he saw a door slightly ajar, pushed it open and slipped inside.

The room was small and sparsely furnished, with a single bed, a dresser loaded with tin cans, and a small table and chair. Sogge quickly scanned the room for any signs of the occupant, but it appeared to be empty. Maybe homeless people had taken over this place.

He crept to the small window on the far side of the room, peering out. He could hear nothing but his own wheezing.

Sogge let out a sigh of relief and turned to leave the room. As he took his first step, he noticed something on the floor. He looked down and saw a thin trail of blood leading from the door to the bed. He realized with a chill that he had left a trail for his pursuers to follow.

He held his breath, failing to suppress the whisper of, "Oh, shit," that escaped his throat.

The door burst open.

He went for the man's groin in an instant, a sharp boot to his balls.

And then they were struggling, squirming, writhing, locked in a deadly embrace.

He had both hands on the man's wrists, holding his handgun pointing to the ceiling.

They were locked in a fatal pause for what seemed an age.

Then a twist and a turn.

The man tried to scream but Sogge fell backwards with him, crashing to the floor. All the breath left his body.

But he had his arms around the man's throat and pulled and wrenched with all his might.

The man gargled, choking, his boots kicking, pedalling an imaginary bike, until he faltered, gasping, wheezing, and eventually slumped.

Dead.

Sogge lay silent for a long time, the dead weight of the man sprawled on his chest. After a while, he shoved the corpse aside and climbed to his feet.

The man stared up at him, eyes frozen, mouth twisted, his obscene tongue lolling, fat.

A man in a police uniform. Sogge recognized him from the Stovner station. A recent recruit.

Sogge choked back a dry heave and made for the open door.

He kicked something that clattered against the skirting board.

A handgun.

A Heckler & Koch P30 semi-automatic. His weapon that should be locked down in his patrol car. The regulation ran through his mind: *arming of locked-down weapons requires permission from the chief of police or someone designated by him.*

Sogge reached down, pocketed the gun and staggered down the stairs and out to the cold night.

37

Blackwood paced the room, peeking out through the blinds for what must have been the fiftieth time. Still no sign of Larsen.

"Relax," Erik said, gazing at the TV news and nursing a gleaming gold glass of aquavit. "You're making us all nervous."

Blackwood put on a smile for the boy's sake. As if everything was all right. But he longed to be out there. He couldn't stand this waiting.

"How convenient," Erik said.

"What?" Blackwood asked.

Erik didn't look at him. "A hardline fascist who wants to crack down on crime, but who just happens to be backed by a crime baron. The world really is running out of ideas."

The television. On screen a familiar face: the same politician's face from the billboard outside the nightclub, and all over the city. The news ticker bore the name, *Ingrid Borstad*. She seemed to be arriving for a gala event. Cameras flashing as she paused for the press before a terracotta-coloured, twin-towered building, giant and foreboding. Blackwood recognized it from the illustration on the tourist map: the Oslo Rådhus. City Hall.

"Look at her," Erik sneered. "A blonde haired, blue eyed, grinning nazi."

"And you think Prestegård is behind her?"

Erik pointed at the screen. "There he is!"

Blackwood stepped closer and squinted. In the melee of her entourage, almost out of the glare of flashlight, was Rune Prestegård. There was something cold, almost robotic about him. He'd changed into another suit, perhaps because he needed something less associated with the casual assassination order he'd doled out this afternoon.

Blackwood thought hard. It was all starting to form a clear picture. A crime boss who wanted to go into politics, to become respectable. Wiping out the competition under the ruse of cleaning up the city. This clean-up had led to killing Dag's son too, and then the attempt on Martin's life. Because Martin had been set up as the killer and was supposed to have died in what would look like teenage gang members shooting each other.

This was why Prestegård's men had shot Dag Engelson last night. Because Dag was smuggling contraband for a rival gang. But the only way to prove that was to find the paintings in the possession of Kjetil Bergstad or Rune Prestegård.

He had an idea. He pulled out his phone and searched for *stolen Munch paintings*. A BBC news feature came up about the heist in a St. Petersburg gallery. There were photos of the three paintings. Gloomy snowscapes, dark and brooding, devoid of life.

They were not the paintings he'd seen in Rune Prestegård's house. Nothing like them.

But it was beyond doubt now that Rune Prestegård was involved in the theft of the paintings and all the murders around them. It was only a matter of whether the police were also involved, and which police.

But Martin had seen his assassin, and whoever it was, he wasn't one of Prestegård's mob. It was more likely the police plant.

"Erik, you said earlier that someone close to Kari had…"

Erik tore his eyes from the television and glanced at Martin.

The boy cast his eyes downward and mumbled, "It's okay."

"I don't know about that," Erik said.

"Come on, you seemed certain this afternoon. It was someone in the force, wasn't it?"

Erik twisted his neck, slumped back in his armchair, and said, "I think so. I have no proof."

"But you must have something."

Erik shook his head.

"Martin. The man who shot at you this morning. The man who tried to kill you. Was it Sogge?"

Martin shook his head.

"Do you recognize the shooter from any of your mother's colleagues?"

"I don't know any of them," Martin said.

Blackwood bit his thumb and paced some more. Of course, there was the possibility that Kari Larsen's husband had been one of those corrupt cops. It was a possibility he'd been thinking of since he'd seen the man's photo.

Erik picked up the poker and prodded the burning wood in the fire grate. A log collapsed into cinders.

"I wonder if you have photos of the police force, Erik," Blackwood said. "I thought it was the kind of thing you might have, seeing as you've been putting this investigation together. Maybe Martin can have a look at them. Maybe he'll see the shooter. It's all we have."

Erik pondered and prodded the fire some more, reluctant to commit himself. His phone bleeped, sitting on the arm of the chair. He snatched it up and squinted at it.

Blackwood flinched at the faint sound of footsteps crunching through the snow outside. He raised a finger to his lips, crept to the window and peered out into the night.

"It's your mother," Erik said.

Blackwood peered closer at the figure emerging from the darkness. Yes, it was Larsen, marching to the cottage with a determined stride.

Erik placed his phone back down on the arm of the chair. He must have a motion detector. Cameras that alerted him to anyone approaching. He'd known who it was before Blackwood had even heard her.

Martin rushed to the door and opened it and fell into his mother's embrace.

She crumpled to her knees, holding onto her son, her hands roaming over him, checking he was all still there.

Fighting back tears, she squeezed him till he moaned in pain.

"I'm okay!" the boy protested.

"Martin, tell me. How close were you to danger?" Larsen asked, her voice trembling.

Blackwood stepped closer and said, "He was fine. I protected him."

Martin nodded and said, "It's okay. It was like a car chase out of a film. But the bullets all missed me."

Larsen held her son tight for a little longer before finally letting go and standing up. She ran her hands over his face and hair one last time before turning to Blackwood with a questioning glare.

Blackwood held her gaze for what felt like an eternity before finally saying, "Your son was never in any real danger. I had it under control."

Larsen's eyes searched Blackwood's face, her expression unreadable. Blackwood couldn't tell whether she was relieved or angry, or perhaps both.

"He nearly died," she said, and slapped Blackwood hard across his cheek.

He recoiled, stunned.

"Kari!" Erik exclaimed. "He saved Martin!"

Larsen stepped closer to Blackwood, seething with suspicion and distrust. "What happened in the north?" she asked sternly. "What happened in the Finnmark?"

"What do you mean?" Blackwood said, turning from her, as much to hide his shame as to stop seeing the hate in her.

"They said it was a border incident. Several murders. Was it a gang turf war, or are you a spy? What the hell are you, Owen Blake?"

Blackwood stroked his stinging cheek. "Look, I was just in the wrong place at--"

"Don't you dare say that!" she screamed, swiping at him again.

Blackwood jerked away from her. "I got into a situation. Rather like this one. Bad people doing bad things to good people. Innocent people. I helped them. Just like I helped you."

"No one needs your help!" she cried.

Erik stepped between them. "Kari, please. Owen wasn't responsible for Martin getting involved with these dangerous people. He saved him from them."

Larsen scowled and spat out, "My son is not safe around a man like you!"

Blackwood swallowed the hurt. It was there for a moment, just a moment, before he replied with as much calm as he could muster. "I saved your son's life. And you also said today that you believed I was a good man."

"Yes, I said that," Larsen said. "But now I'm not so sure. You are a killer. A killer whose real name I don't even know."

Blackwood stared at her unflinchingly and said in a low voice, "We all have secrets. Things in our past we don't like to talk about."

"What is that supposed to mean?" she demanded.

"Why don't you tell me about your husband and whether he was on the take?"

Larsen stormed forward and slapped him once more. His cheek burned but he did not flinch. He kept his gaze steady on hers as she spoke.

"Martin's father was a good man," she hissed.

"But you aren't sure, are you?" Blackwood said. "Just like with me."

Larsen's eyes narrowed as she glared at Blackwood. "You have no right to bring up my husband. He is dead and gone."

Blackwood stood his ground. "I'm sorry, but you have to understand that I need to know everything about the people I work with."

"Work with?" Larsen sneered. "I never hired you. You just showed up and started meddling in our lives."

Blackwood took a step closer. "You needed my help, and I gave it to you. I saved your son's life and you know it. Now, if you want my help again, you need to trust me."

Larsen shook her head. "I don't know if I can," she said, her voice barely above a whisper.

Blackwood stepped back, his eyes scanning the room. He knew he had pushed too hard, but he also knew that Larsen needed him, whether she knew it or not. He needed to earn her trust, and quickly.

"I understand," Blackwood said. "But there's something you need to know. There are people out there who want to hurt you and your family. And it's not just the criminals you pursue every day. It's your own people."

Larsen whispered, "What do you mean?" But her tone betrayed she knew exactly.

"The people who took your son. The people who chased us and shot at us. It wasn't just the criminals. It was the police too. They won't stop until they get what they want. I can protect you, but I need your cooperation."

"What do you think they want?" she asked.

"I don't know yet," Blackwood admitted. "But I'll find out. And when I do, I'll make sure they never bother you again."

Blackwood's phone rang. He dug it out of his jacket pocket and answered with an apprehensive "Hello?"

"It's Kalland," the voice said. "I've got something from this little device I acquired today."

"Excellent," Blackwood said. "Tell me."

"I can't say it over the phone."

"Oh?" Blackwood questioned, his tone dubious.

"We need to meet in person."

Blackwood paused for a moment. Was this safe; it might it be a trap; could Kalland be leading the police right to him? Maybe not. He wanted in on the whole story and seemed like a reliable campaigning journalist who just wanted the dirt.

"Why don't you suggest where we can meet safely?" Blackwood said.

38

Kari Larsen listened, not breathing, as soon as Owen Blake left the cabin, his footsteps sloshing through snow, until his stolen car ignited and roared off. She waited till it was gone before turning to the room.

Erik was watching her sadly.

Martin seemed hypnotized by the television, but she was sure he wasn't really watching it. Ingrid Borstad's too perfect face filled the screen, her blue eyes sparkling with just a little too much psychotic energy. The face of a woman that would turn men's heads, but you wouldn't invite her into your home. You knew she would destroy it.

Larsen breathed again and clutched her heart. Martin's safety was all that mattered now.

"Are you all right, Kari?"

She turned to Erik, her piercing gaze locking onto him. "We need to get out of here."

"Why?" Erik asked. But he knew.

"Martin needs protection," she said, her voice urgent but hushed. "I want you to take him somewhere safe."

Martin turned from the television now. "Why, mom?"

"Because it's not safe here. You're not safe."

"Where?" Erik asked, his brow furrowing.

"Somewhere unknown. This place is compromised." Larsen's determination shone through her fear.

Erik nodded, swallowing hard. He glanced at Martin. The boy's eyes revealed a terror he tried to conceal.

Larsen's maternal instincts kicked in full force. She leaned down, pulling Martin into a tight embrace as he sat in the armchair. "Listen, sweetheart. Erik's going to keep you safe, okay? I'll be back as soon as I can."

Martin's quivering voice broke her heart. "Promise?"

"Promise." She squeezed him tighter, then released her grip.

"What are you going to do?" Erik asked. "You're going to go with Owen, yes?"

Larsen shook her head. "I don't trust him. I want him away from all of us."

"But Kari, he saved Martin."

Larsen's eyes narrowed. "He's not who he says he is. Fake ID, dangerous past. And he's been at the heart of every single death today."

"Blake is our best shot." Erik met her gaze, hoping to convey his sincerity. "Think about it."

She clenched her fists. "I can't trust anyone. Not now. Only you. Tell me you have somewhere you can go. Somewhere no one knows about."

"I know a place," Erik said, reluctance in his voice.

"Just go. Now."

Erik nodded and looked around the room, then sprang into action with a sudden determination. In steady, practised movements, he zapped off the television and shut down his computers. The hum of machinery faded, leaving only silence in its wake.

"Where are we going?" Martin asked, his voice small and scared.

"Don't tell me about it," Larsen barked.

"Somewhere safe." Erik's eyes never left the screens as they went dark. He grabbed a mobile flash drive and laptop, tossing them into a bag with swift precision, then reached under the desk and pulled something away and shoved it into his overcoat pocket. He had prepared for this, many times.

Martin shrugged into his puffa jacket and pulled his woolly hat over his blonde curls.

"Time's up," Larsen snapped, feeling the weight of the world on her shoulders.

"Let's do it," Erik said, as he led Martin out into the cold night.

Larsen followed them out, her heart pounding in her chest.

They paused at Erik's car and turned to her, the raw fear in them both that they were seeing her for the last time. She hugged Erik.

"Remember, Kari," he whispered, "it's our own people working with Prestegård. Not Blake."

"Right," she muttered. That just meant no one could be trusted.

She pulled Martin towards her and hugged him violently, then pushed him away. "Stay safe. I'll see you soon." She bit her lip, fighting back tears.

"Stay safe too, Mamma." Martin climbed into the car.

"Take care of my son," Larsen whispered, her words barely audible.

Erik took the pistol from his coat pocket and held it silently for a moment, so she could see it and understand. Larsen nodded.

And with that, he slung the bag into the car and climbed in.

Larsen watched them go, her heart heavy with doubt and fear.

"Stay safe," she murmured into the night, her breath forming clouds in the cold.

Inside her car, she gripped the steering wheel, knuckles turning white, and roared out of that compound, turning left down the mountainside and the dark road back to Oslo.

Her phone rang, piercing the silence. Henrik Haaken's name flashed across the screen. What did the Detective Chief Inspector want now? She hesitated, then answered.

"Larsen, where are you?" His voice was ice-cold and sharp.

"Why? What's up?" she asked.

"Just tell me where you are."

The windscreen wipers swiped a message with an insistent whisper. *Don't you trust him, don't you trust him, don't you trust him...*

"Er, difficult to say," she said.

"What do you mean? Just tell m—"

"I'm in transit."

She hung up, fingers trembling. Trust evaporated like mist. The car raced forward, as if sensing her urgency.

39

A five-minute stroll from the Dagbladet office in the Halse end of Grünerløkka, Blackwood found the Shamrock Pub, lit by dim green neon: a street corner bar behind a front beer garden fenced off with green planks and leafless trees.

Blackwood hesitated at the entrance, surveying the area. No immediate threats, but that meant nothing. The danger could come from anywhere.

He pushed open the door, stepping inside, the warmth of the place hitting him like a wave. He scanned the room, taking note of the patrons sitting at the bar and the tables along the walls. A modest, quiet crowd, despite the music blaring and the football on screens all over the pub. A few people were sitting at the tables scattered around the room, talking quietly among themselves.

As he walked to the bar, he caught the eye of the bartender, a tall, muscular man with a shaved head and tattoos on his arms. The man nodded at him but didn't say anything. Blackwood noticed a group of men in the corner, their faces obscured by the shadows. He couldn't tell if they were a threat or not.

He placed both hands on the bar, aware of the gun digging into the small of his back, and scanned the shelf of whiskey bottles. To his surprise they only had two Irish whiskeys, Jamesons and Tullamore Dew, nothing interesting, so he ordered a Lagavulin 16-year-old and nosed it with sensual delight, forgetting everything for a moment, lost at sea on a burning ship.

His phone vibrated in his pocket, just the once. He dug it out to find a text message from Kalland.

Back corner.

Blackwood strolled through the pub, veering towards a side section where a pool table lay quiet. Kalland was at a lone table in a shadowy corner, back against the wall. His eyes locked onto Blackwood's.

"Kalland." Blackwood nodded as he reached the table.

"Owen," Kalland replied, a hint of urgency in his voice.

"An Irish pub. Really?"

"That is your nationality, isn't it? According to your passport."

Blackwood laughed and shook his head.

Kalland frowned and took a laptop from his satchel. Not Prestegård's dented laptop. This was a smaller, more compact device, the size of a tablet but with a keyboard. A leather pouch the size of a mobile phone was plugged into the laptop with a small, black cable.

Kalland caught Blackwood's puzzled look and smirked. "I took the hard drive out of Prestegård's laptop."

Blackwood nodded.

Kalland turned the laptop at an angle so they could both view the screen. A chaotic digital spread of evidence. Blackwood's eyes flicked over each piece, processing the information. Photos of famous art works, of galleries, news stories of robberies, detailed inventories of the artworks. Lists of international art dealers.

"This looks like surveillance," Kalland said. "The gallery photos, the information on the paintings. Every one of these paintings was stolen. These are the sort of art dealers who are, you might say, kind of grey. The guys you might expect to facilitate the deals only very private and very rich collectors might be interested in."

"Is Jakob Varg on the list?"

Kalland looked surprised, scrolled back and forth, and found it. "Yes. Yes, he is."

"He was murdered a couple of days ago in his house in Bergen."

"How do you know?"

"I saw him two hours ago. The police should be dealing with the body now."

Kalland pulled up another page. It seemed to be a Dagbladet internal bulletin feed. He nodded. "Yes, there it is. Just happened. He's dead?"

"We think he was murdered by a police contact. A corrupt cop who's involved in all of this."

"So, all of this, on Prestegård's laptop, is evidence of his involvement in art heists?"

"Not just any old art heist," Blackwood said, tapping a finger on the table. "*The* heist. The one everyone is talking about."

Kalland whistled. "That's quite a story."

"Is all of this solid?" Blackwood pointed to the screen. "I mean it's not just circumstantial?"

Kalland grimaced. "I don't know. A top lawyer could probably get him off even if he had the paintings hanging in his house."

Blackwood took another sip of Lagavulin and pondered.

Kalland said, "Rune Prestegård offered a reward for the return of the Munch paintings. And you think he stole them himself? That's quite a move."

"It's all about dirty money," Blackwood said. "Stolen art funds their drive for respectability. And look, right this minute, he's side by side with that politician who's taking power."

"So the gang turns legitimate," Kalland cooed. "It's all a façade. All a mask to hide the truth."

Blackwood stared with dumbfounded wonder.

Of course. That was it.

Then his fists clenched. Dag's face flashed in his mind, the worried look he'd given him as he got out of the cab this morning, moments before he was shot dead. Poor Gunilla, his widow, who was probably still crying, still broken. And Martin, shaking with fear. All of these innocents drawn into this, their lives counting for nothing. He exhaled sharply, anger simmering beneath the surface. "Damn them."

Blackwood knocked back the last of the Lagavulin and stood, muscles coiled with purpose, the Kahr P9 cold in the small of his back.

"Hey, what are you going to do?"

"Something reckless."

"Watch out," Kalland said. "These are dangerous men."

"So am I."

Blackwood left, each stride fuelled by urgency. The night air stung his face, but he barely felt it. A storm brewing inside him, ready to break loose.

40

Larsen clenched her fists as she approached the Oslo Rådhus. The sprawling building loomed above, floodlit in the falling snow. A crowd had gathered outside, their eager faces illuminated by the glow of camera phones, awaiting Ingrid Borstad's victory speech.

Larsen pushed through the throng, wondering what the hell she was going to do. Arrest Ingrid Borstad as the architect behind today's murders? Confront her with the accusation and hope she broke down and confessed?

"Move!" Kari barked, shoving a man holding a *Borstad for Change* sign.

"Hey, bitch!" he exclaimed, but Larsen was already gone, focused on reaching the security entrance.

"ID," demanded the burly guard, his eyes cold and unyielding.

She flashed her police ID without hesitation. No one here would know she was suspended. Not yet. And suspended or not, she was still a detective.

The guard nodded, allowing her passage into the restricted area.

"Thanks," she muttered, marching through.

Beyond security, the atmosphere buzzed with anticipation. Handlers and assistants scurried about, preparing for the imminent celebration. Kari spotted Borstad in the distance, her immaculate blonde hair a beacon amidst the chaos. She was surrounded by her entourage, each step carefully orchestrated.

Larsen advanced, her heart pounding in her chest.

"Excuse me," Kari said, stepping in front of Borstad, her voice trembling with barely contained emotion. "We need to talk."

Borstad's eyes met Larsen's, a flicker of recognition crossing her face.

"Your connection to the crime gang. I know about it," Larsen said, her voice low and fierce. She pointed towards Rune Prestegård, lurking among Borstad's entourage like a snake in the grass. "He's one of them."

Borstad's blue eyes narrowed, but her smile never faltered. Cameras flashed around them, preserving this moment for the world to see.

"Detective Sergeant Larsen, is it?" She tilted her head, feigning concern. "You seem to be quite mistaken. I'm here to address the criminal corruption in our city, not to perpetuate it."

Larsen clenched her fists.

Borstad's words were poison, laced with charm and confidence. She could feel the cameras capturing their exchange, the weight of public scrutiny bearing down on her.

"Are you denying your association with Prestegård?" Larsen pressed, her gaze unwavering.

"Of course not." Borstad's laugh was light and carefree, a stark contrast to the gravity of the situation. "Rune Prestegård is a respectable businessman who shares my concerns for the crimewave gripping our city. A crimewave you police have failed to deal with."

Larsen's mind raced, trying to find the right words to expose Borstad's lies. But as she searched, the politician continued speaking, her voice rising above the noise of the bustling room.

"Tonight, we celebrate the beginning of a new era," Borstad announced, addressing the crowd now gathered around them. "An era free from the grip of criminal corruption!"

Larsen's heart sank. It was happening – Borstad was winning, and there was nothing she could do to stop it.

"Your charade won't last, Borstad," Larsen spat, gathering the last of her courage. "There's evidence coming to light – proof that you're connected to drug gangs and the murders in this city today."

Borstad's laughter was cold, dismissive. "Oh, Detective Sergeant Larsen, is that so?" Her eyes narrowed, predatory. "I heard a rumour that it's actually your son who's involved with these gangs. Just like his deceased father."

Larsen's heart hammered in her chest, icy fear snaking up her spine. She hissed through gritted teeth, struggling to control her trembling fists that wanted to punch Ingrid Borstad's face in. "You leave my son alone or I'll…"

"Is that a threat I hear, Detective?" Borstad taunted, savouring Kari's distress. "It must run in the family."

Larsen's vision blurred with rage, the room spinning around her. "You fucking—"

But before she could say another word, burly arms encircled her, yanking her away from the politician. She tried to resist, but their grip was unyielding, her strength fading.

As they dragged her back, Kari spotted her boss Haaken and Superintendent Kjell Thorstad. The two tall men approaching through the crowd. Their eyes about to land on her.

Panic swelled in her throat. They couldn't see her like this, not now. Not when everything was at stake.

The world narrowed down to the sound of her own heartbeat as the security guards pushed her back.

Moments later she stumbled outside, the cold Oslo air hitting her like a slap. Her breath hitched as she fought back tears, her world crumbling around her.

The crowd roared, a tsunami of sound as Borstad emerged from the Rådhus, waving to her adoring supporters.

"Oslo will be great again!" Borstad shouted.

The voters ate it up, chanting her name.

"Get out of my way!" Larsen snapped, shoving through the throng. Hands grabbed at her, but she shook them off, desperate for escape, eventually pushing through to the edge of the crowd, and the bleak, forlorn city.

"Kari!" a voice yelled.

She turned and looked back to see a figure pushing through the crowd, a man fighting waves, near to drowning, his pale face contorted with fury.

It was Sogge.

She turned and ran as fast as she could across iced paving. Everyone in the city was against her. She didn't look back till she was streets away and absolutely certain that Sogge had not trailed her.

41

Reaching the nondescript sedan, Blackwood unlocked the door with practised ease. He slid into the driver's seat. The engine roared to life, momentarily drowning out the chaos inside his head. Blackwood gripped the steering wheel tightly, feeling its worn leather beneath his calloused fingertips. His eyes scanned the dark streets, calculating the best route to his destination.

It was simple.

Find the paintings.

End this.

He knew exactly where he needed to go.

The city blurred by, a cacophony of neon and darkness. Blackwood's eyes locked onto the billboards that towered above the street, illuminated faces staring down at him. There she was – Ingrid Borstad, her political campaign slogans a riot of diacritical and exclamation marks. The same woman Erik had seethed at on TV, with Rune Prestegård by her side at the rally.

His phone buzzed, jolting him from his reverie. Larsen's name flashed across the screen. He hesitated for a second before answering.

"Where are you?" Her voice was curt, betraying her concern.

"I've just left Kalland," Blackwood replied. "He gave me new intel."

"Like what?" she demanded.

"Later," Blackwood said, his gaze flickering between the rearview mirror and the road ahead. "I'm closing in on them."

He could feel Larsen's distrust like a stone in his gut, but he couldn't let it slow him down.

"Owen," Larsen's voice crackled through the phone, her tone icy. "You'd better tell me what you're doing."

"Thought you were done with me," Blackwood countered, his eyes locked onto the road ahead. "Didn't need me anymore, remember?"

"Trust doesn't come easy," she snapped, her voice wavering ever so slightly. "I can't trust anyone. Not in this world."

"Except Erik," Blackwood reminded her, the name like a lifeline in the darkness.

There was a pause, and Blackwood could hear the uneasy shift in Larsen's breathing. "Yes," she finally admitted. "Erik is the only one I trust. He has my son, Martin. They're safe, for now."

"Then you should know," Blackwood said, his words measured and deliberate. "Erik told you to trust me, didn't he?"

Silence filled the line, punctuated by the steady hum of the engine and Blackwood's own pulse thundering in his ears. He knew how difficult it was for her to place her faith in a stranger, but time was running out.

"Look, I'm the only person trying to help you right now," Blackwood shot back, his voice a low growl. "I don't need to be here. I can turn this car around and be gone, out of Oslo. I can be gone like that."

"No," she sighed, her defences crumbling. "Just... Tell me where you're going."

The car slowed, and Blackwood let the engine idle as he gazed upon Rune Prestegård's house, tall and imposing, soaking up the shadows cast by the moonlight.

42

The lights were out, and that made sense. Prestegård was at the Rådhus if the TV pictures were telling the truth. An ornate wrought-iron fence bordered the front of the property.

The rear of the property, he knew, was rather different. That head-high wall and the length of garden, and a shattered plate glass window that was now boarded up with a stud wall.

Blackwood opened the pizza box on his lap and swooned at the smell that filled the car. He hadn't eaten since... when? Perhaps this morning when he'd stocked up on fuel.

He took a couple of slices of pizza and scoffed them down, burning the roof of his mouth. It didn't matter.

He closed the box, stepped out of the car and, steeling himself, marched across the street to the gate, just as if he was the guy that came here to deliver pizza any other night.

He bent over the lock and jemmied it with a few jabs of his penknife. It was no security at all, and anyone observing would think he was waiting for the intercom to buzz him through.

The gate creaked open, he pushed it to behind him, but not locked, and strode up the path to the front door, disappearing into the shadow provided by the ostentatious portico.

The front door would not be as easy to pick, but he dropped the pizza box at his feet and tried both locks. Sixty seconds of awkward, silent fiddling and the door eased open. Noiselessly, he slipped inside.

The skylight above the grand staircase illuminated the dark hallway in spectral light. A single, red light winked above and Blackwood gazed on it, unfazed. A security camera. It was no doubt alarmed. Nothing so vulgar as a blaring burglar alarm for Rune Prestegård. Just a simple, silent warning relayed to his phone, or that of his security.

He had about five minutes before they came.

But that didn't matter. That was part of the plan.

No need to go upstairs, as he had this morning. He knew exactly where the paintings were.

To the right of the great hallway, the enormous living room space, minimal and tastefully designed, almost like an art gallery.

And there were the three pictures that hung on the wall. Kitsch and tasteless. He'd noticed them this morning and wondered how a gangster like Prestegård could buy the best of everything, but not taste.

There was no safe behind any of the pictures. He'd checked that. But the valuables weren't in any safe, he was sure. This time, he ran his thumb along the ornate picture frame, looking for something. He wasn't sure what. A catch, a button, something that would…

A gear clicked and whirred and the painting glided up in its frame, disappearing into the top frame, no doubt curling into a roll. It revealed something that was not kitsch and tasteless. Something that looked decidedly tasteful, and valuable.

A rough canvas landscape in thick oil. Swathes of white, brown and blue. A dark, brooding snowscape.

The other two picture frames sat around the room, guarding their secrets. Blackwood wondered at the thinking behind it all. Larsen had said that criminals used stolen art as easy currency and it was often recovered in a damaged state because the criminals didn't give a shit about art. They just rolled a priceless canvas up in a plastic bag and hid it under floorboards in a barn. But this was different. Prestegård had invested in keeping the paintings in good condition, even framed respectfully in his house.

That was it. It was an ego thing, a status thing.

Prestegård would not sell the paintings, use them as easy currency just like every other small-time criminal. He would recover them and be a national hero. But first he would indulge in the pleasure of having a house filled with old masters. He would sit on that sofa, sipping that whisky, and stare at his masterpieces, luxuriating in the sheer greedy pleasure of possessing them.

With a sneer of disgust, Blackwood pressed the hidden button on each picture frame. The fake, kitsch canvases of sad clowns rolled back into place, hiding Edvard Munch's snowscapes once more.

Blackwood took the Kahr P9 from his belt. He checked the clip, even though he knew. Five rounds left.

He checked his wristwatch.

Perhaps only another minute before they came.

43

Blackwood went to the drinks cabinet and poured himself a Johnny Walker Blue Label. A finger of amber in a fat, crystal glass.

He sat on the leather sofa, sipping liquid gold, and waited.

The lights were out, leaving only the faint glow of moonlight filtering in through the tall windows. He closed his eyes, ears attuned to the slightest noise. That's when he heard it — the unmistakable sound of footsteps approaching.

The gate creaked. Their boots crumped up the path, unable to avoid making a noise on the snow. They reached the front door and stepped inside and that was when one of them kicked the pizza box he'd dropped by the door.

The soft cardboard crumpled beneath the force. Blackwood's lips curled into a grim smile. They had no idea what they were walking into. He kept his breathing steady, controlling the flood of adrenalin.

A hushed command came from one of the intruders. Something in Norwegian.

Blackwood rose and crossed the room, crouching behind a pillar. The stolen paintings were just a few feet away. He watched as the leader of the gang stepped into the room, Glock 17 poking out in front of him. Kjetil Bergman's profile was unmistakable, and Blackwood guessed he was still sore from the beating he'd taken this morning. Sore and angry.

Another two followed suit, their weapons poised and ready to fire.

But they wouldn't fire, Blackwood reckoned.

This was Rune Prestegård's mansion. It had already suffered a great deal of damage today and his gang coming in shooting the place up was unlikely.

"Come on out!" Kjetil Bergman yelled, in English, his eyes darting around the dimly lit room.

So he knew it was Blackwood. Prestegård had probably warned them that he would return.

Blackwood's heart pounded in his chest, but he remained still, waiting for the perfect moment to strike.

He had to take the fight away from this room with the paintings.

As Kjetil Bergman probed forward, Blackwood sprinted at him, catching the man off guard with a swift kick to the chest. His gun skidded across the floor, lost in the shadows. Bergman crumpled and a boot in his face had him screaming in pain for the second time today.

Before he could fall to the floor, Blackwood snatched him, turned him round and shoved him at the man running towards them.

Their heads cracked. The man howled and grabbed his broken nose. Blackwood disarmed him with a powerful blow to the wrist. The gunman cried out in pain, dropping his weapon to the ground.

More men were piling into the room, silhouetted in the doorway, afraid to shoot.

Moving swiftly and silently, Blackwood made for the second door and crossed into the hallway.

They heard his footsteps and scurried to chase him.

Blackwood circled back to the first door, anticipating the man who'd come in last would come running out of the main room.

One gang member rounded each corner and advanced on him, their faces twisted into snarls.

The fight had moved to the hallway, lit in spectral moonlight.

Blackwood quickly assessed their stances — one had a background in boxing, while the other seemed to favour a rougher street fighting style. Neither would be an easy opponent, but Blackwood had faced worse odds before.

The boxer lunged first, throwing a vicious right hook aimed at Blackwood's jaw. Blackwood ducked under the punch, using the momentum to drive his shoulder into the man's gut. The wind left the attacker's lungs in a whoosh as he crumpled to the ground, yawning for air.

An elbow to the temple made sure the man stayed out cold.

Blackwood didn't have time to celebrate his small victory; the street fighter was already upon him, launching a barrage of wild swings and kicks.

Blackwood deflected each strike, countering with precise jabs and knee strikes designed to disable rather than kill.

He drove his fist into the street fighter's kidney. The man gasped in pain, staggering back from the blow. Blackwood pressed his advantage, grappling with the man and using his superior strength to force him against the wall.

The street fighter spat, blood flecking Blackwood's face. His eyes held a wild desperation that Blackwood recognized all too well — the determination to fight until the bitter end.

Blackwood headbutted him with a single vicious crack of bone.

As the body slumped to the floor, he took a moment to catch his breath, steeling himself for the next round of combat.

Four men in total, and all of them recovering and getting to their feet, reaching for their guns.

Blackwood darted to the rear and the vast kitchen where he'd broken in this morning.

The window wall was boarded up and the room steeped in darkness. But he remembered the line of knives hanging on a magnetic strip. He snatched one up and waited.

It was Kjetil Bergman who blundered in, Glock 17 raised, but he didn't anticipate his prey pounding towards him and diving into a roll that took his legs from under him.

His head smacked into the parquet floor.

Blackwood kicked the Glock away. It skidded across the floor and clattered into the chipboard that covered the broken window.

Bergman rose, fury burning him up.

Their eyes locked. Bergman saw the knife glinting in Blackwood's fist and snatched one from the wall.

They circled each other in the dimly lit room, their breathing heavy, sweat dripping from their brows.

Bergman lunged first.

Their blades clashed, the sound echoing through the house.

Blackwood parried Bergman's wild swings, focusing all his energy on finding an opening.

In a moment, Blackwood saw his chance. He sidestepped a poorly aimed swing and drove his knee into Bergman's gut. The gang leader doubled over, gasping for air. Blackwood twisted his arm, forcing his enemy to drop the knife.

"Last chance," Blackwood warned, his voice cold and unforgiving.

"Go to hell," Bergman wheezed, defiance burning in his eyes.

"Already been there," Blackwood muttered, snapping Bergman's arm with a swift, brutal motion.

The man howled in pain.

In a moment, Blackwood marched out of the kitchen, back to the hall and pounded up the stairs, the groaning assailants gathering themselves from the floor.

The landing up there was illuminated by the skylight. The room at the end where they'd tortured him this morning was open. Blackwood went the other way, his steps obscured by their clumsy boots pounding up the marble stairs, shouting taunts and orders in Norwegian.

Blackwood snatched up a vase from a faux Greek marble dais and launched it towards the far end of the landing. It crashed by the open door to the rear room: Rune Prestegård's office.

The men crept up the stairs, their handguns before them.

A tense silence descended on the opulent mansion.

They crept to the top of the stairs and inched towards Prestegård's office, not even looking back to where Blackwood stood, watching, waiting. Every one of them following the sound of the shattered vase. Docile, stupid amateurs.

This was the moment.

In the end, no matter how hard you tried, it always came down to this.

It always came down to death.

Blackwood gripped the cold metal of his Kahr P9, the weight of the handgun familiar and comforting in his hand.

It would be easy to pick them off, shoot them in the back. It would be over in moments, before any of them had the chance to shoot back, even turn and see their prey.

Larsen had said 'No killing'. How was that even possible, here, in this place, with these men?

"Shit!" Blackwood hissed.

He couldn't do it.

He'd shot men like that before. Men who didn't see it coming. One moment breathing, the next moment gone, blank, nothing.

He was done with that.

But it seemed Death kept pulling him back, beguiling, taunting, like a jilted lover desperate to be needed again.

He lowered the Kahr P9.

Something about the movement, perhaps his whispered curse carried on the air, finally reached them. Or perhaps the realisation that he was not in the back office and they'd been tricked. All of that, perhaps, made the men turn and face him.

The first shot rang out.

44

As Larsen's car cut through the frigid Oslo night, streetlights bathed the snow-covered roads with their orange glow, casting long shadows that slithered around her vehicle. The dull ache of despair, defeat, throbbed across her breast. Just then, her phone pierced the quiet with a shrill ring.

"Haaken," she muttered under her breath, recognizing the number on the screen.

Had he seen her at the Rådhus? Or maybe Ingrid Borstad had informed him of their encounter. Reluctantly, she tapped the Bluetooth button on her wheel.

"Where are you, Larsen?" Haaken barked, his voice grating like nails on a chalkboard.

"Last I checked, I'm suspended," she spat back, the words tasting bitter on her tongue.

"Well, yes," his voice came back. "But I need to know where you are."

"Why?"

This was not the voice of someone who knew she'd abused her position and ID to interrogate a politician. Haaken didn't know she'd questioned Borstad and hadn't seen her at the Rådhus, she was certain.

A brief pause settled between them before Haaken's tone softened. "We've located Sogge. I'm telling you this for your own safety."

Larsen's heart skipped a beat. A mixture of relief and dread washed over her as Haaken's words sank in. They must have tried to apprehend Sogge at the Rådhus. Just after he'd shouted at her in the rally crowd; maybe he'd tried to get into the building. Owen Blake's warning echoed in her mind: Sogge was dangerous. The thought of him lurking in the shadows, waiting for an opportunity to strike; the man who had hunted down her son earlier today.

"Listen, Larsen," Haaken's voice cut through her thoughts, pulling her back to reality. "I need you to be present at the scene of the arrest."

"You don't have him?"

"We've located him. We're about to arrest him."

"Where?" she asked, her pulse quickening.

"The Karakkevik bar in Bryn. Teo Molund's territory."

Streetlights glinted off the icy pavement, casting shadows that seemed to reach out for her.

So they'd tried to apprehend Sogge at the Rådhus, and he'd somehow escaped and high-tailed it to Bryn and Teo Molund's lair.

"Fine," Larsen snapped into the phone. "I'll be there in an hour."

"An hour is too late..." Haaken snapped.

She hung up and put her foot down. The car's engine growled beneath her as she accelerated, the snow crunching beneath the tyres. The streets blurred past, a tapestry of darkness dotted with the occasional streetlight.

It didn't make sense.

How could Sogge be involved with Molund's gang when it was Molund himself who had tipped her off about the stolen paintings? And why was she heading in the opposite direction?

Because she needed to find out why Sogge had betrayed her. And she needed to discover the truth about Owen Blake.

The car's heater blasted warm air, but it did little to chase away the chill creeping through her body. The night seemed darker than ever, the snowstorm swallowing everything in its path.

Larsen's car skidded to a stop outside Rune Prestegård's house.

Snowflakes danced in the beams of her headlights and stuck to the windshield as she scrutinized the darkened windows of the residence. Something was off. A flicker of unease gnawed at her gut.

She scanned her surroundings and took a deep breath, steeling herself.

Stepping out of the car, the icy wind bit into her exposed skin. Her boots crunched through the fresh snow as she approached the front gate. She paused for a moment, straining to hear any movement inside the dark house.

Nothing.

The silence was deafening.

The gate was not locked.

She pushed at it and it groaned open.

And that was when the shooting began.

45

THE LOUD CRACK OF a Beretta echoed through the mansion.

The faux Greek marble dais exploded, spraying shards of cheap plaster all over Blackwood.

He dropped to a crouch, squeezing off a single shot with his Kahr P9.

The man with the Beretta fell to the floor like a sack of meat.

And then the plush landing was a firing range, deafening. Glass shattered and wood splintered as bullets tore through the air.

Blackwood shot another couple of rounds, aiming for the muzzle flashes, aware that he would use up the clip any second, cursing himself for not having picked up any of their guns when he'd disabled them moments earlier.

Two of the men fell.

Another screamed and catapulted over the banister to crash down to the hallway.

And now it was just Kjetil Bergman's Glock 17 barking angrily in response.

"Fucking English!" he roared, aiming at Blackwood's position.

Blackwood rolled to the side, miraculously avoiding being hit.

Last bullet.

He aimed and squeezed.

A picture on the wall behind Kjetil Bergman exploded.

Blackwood sprang to his feet and threw the Kahr P9.

Bergman ducked but the gun bounced off his skull. He shot back. The gun clicked, empty. *"Ficken!"* he screamed, and came running.

Blackwood ran to meet him where the marble stairs swept down to the grand hallway.

Bergman lunged at Blackwood with a fury born of desperation. "Die!" he screamed, his fists flying.

Blackwood narrowly dodged the assault, countering with a swift elbow to the man's jaw.

Bergman stumbled back, only to come right back at Blackwood again.

He was relentless, pushing Blackwood back with a flurry of punches and kicks.

Blackwood grabbed an arm as Bergman went in for another punch, using the momentum to throw him.

Despite the wall shuddering under the impact, Bergman recovered. He leaped at Blackwood with renewed vigour.

Blackwood was ready this time, blocking a punch, retaliating with a kick that swept Bergman off his feet.

Bergman scrambled back up and charged like a mad bull, delivering punishing blows as he tried desperately to get past his guard.

Blackwood blocked each one until finally he had an opening. A momentary lapse in Bergman's defence.

The uppercut sent the man sprawling against the banister. He tottered, almost going over, arms windmilling to keep his balance.

Rage gripped Blackwood. This was the man who had shot Dag Engelson this morning. Shot him dead like an animal.

Blackwood saw his chance. He flew at Bergman, sending them both over the banister.

For a breathless moment they floated.

Blackwood twisted, one fist gripping Bergman's shirt, the other arm locked against his throat.

Bergman was under him as they hit the floor.

Blackwood bounced off and smacked into cool marble with a dull thud.

Pain ricocheted through every limb.

He lay, panting, all his senses blurred through a torrent of pain.

He didn't spring up.

Kjetil Bergman wasn't getting up.

Kjetil Bergman was lying, staring at the skylight and the stars over Oslo high above. Stars he didn't even see.

Kjetil Bergman was dead.

The snap of his neck breaking had been louder than the crunches and cracks going through Blackwood's body.

46

The gunshots that rang out from within shattered the stillness of the night.

Larsen's heart slammed against her ribcage, the sound echoing in her ears like thunder. Instinct kicked in. She pressed herself against the wall next to the door, and reached for a weapon that wasn't there.

An eternity seemed to pass before the gunfire ceased. She forced herself to take a deep, steadying breath. This wasn't the time for fear or hesitation – not if lives were at stake.

With one final glance at the silent street behind her, she stepped into the house and skirted immediately to the side, so she wouldn't be silhouetted in the door like a target on the firing range.

The air was heavy with the coppery tang of blood and the stench of cordite. As she surveyed the vast hall, lit by moonlight from the skylight, her thoughts raced, trying to piece together what had happened.

Three bodies prone in the middle of the black and white tiled floor, like a chess game gone very wrong. Two supine. One prone, a pistol still in his hand.

She inched forward, her pulse pounding in her ears.

Another gun lay on the floor, near a pizza box. She snatched it up and felt the comfort of it in her hand. A Glock 17.

A figure stirred among the carnage and sat up.

"Freeze!" Larsen barked, aiming her gun at him.

Owen Blake.

His eyes met hers, filled with a weariness that betrayed his hardened exterior.

"I killed them all," he rasped, raising his hands in surrender. "The whole gang. Sorry."

Larsen hesitated, studying his bruised and battered face.

"Even Bergman?" Larsen asked, her eyes flicking to the lifeless body of the gang leader.

"Especially him." Blake's voice was cold and unyielding.

For a moment, neither of them spoke. Reluctantly, she lowered her weapon and extended a hand to help him up.

Blake grunted in pain as he rose to his feet, leaning heavily on her for support. "The paintings," he said. "I found them."

"Show me," she demanded.

He nodded, limping towards a door that led to the main room.

The room was one of those grand, cold spaces that felt more like an art gallery, or the lobby of an investment bank. Her eyes went to the three paintings that hung on the walls.

"There was something strange about the pictures," Owen Blake said.

"They're awful."

"Yes. I thought it showed just bad taste, but I'm no art expert."

"No, they are truly shit."

"Watch this," Blake said. He limped to one of the pictures and ran his fingers along the ornate golden frame. He fiddled, like he was finding a hidden button. There was a whirring sound and the crass, cheap picture slid away, revealing a dark old oil painting.

Larsen let out a gasp. Even in this low light, she recognized the painting. Edvard Munch's *White Night*. An ironic title as there were only a few specks of white on the canvas, the presiding tone being deep browns and greens and a twilight blue. She switched on the light and leaned in close to take it in, afraid to breathe on it.

Blake went to the other two paintings and found the same trigger switch.

Larsen gasped again as Munch's canvases were revealed. The same paintings she had wondered over twenty years ago in a Copenhagen gallery. *Winter in the Woods* and *Winter on the Fjord*. She felt again the same primal pull of home and belonging.

"My god," she said.

"They're the stolen paintings, aren't they?" Owen Blake said.

She nodded. These were Munch's winter landscapes, without a doubt.

This room, the cold, soulless room, seemed entirely designed for Rune Prestegård to sit and admire his stolen paintings. His own private art gallery of masterpieces.

The arrogance of it galled her. Her hand tightened on the gun in her hand.

And just then, there was a great bang from the rear of the house.

She had heard that sound enough to know what it was: the shattering of a door. A door that had been kicked down.

Blake scurried into the hallway.

She followed, her gun raised ahead of her.

As he ran through the hallway, he snatched up the pistol from the hand of the dead man that lay prone – a Sig Sauer – and darted through to the rear of the house.

She followed him to a vast showroom kitchen.

Blake and another man were pointing guns at each other, and for an instant she didn't know which person to aim at.

Because the man who had kicked through a great square of hardboard was her partner.

Sogge.

47

Larsen looked over Sogge's shoulder to the dark garden behind and verified with a single glance that Sogge was not the spearhead of a unit attack. No one was following him into the house.

The breach, from the rough state of the hardboard kicked through and now leaning at an angle across the kitchen, told of a clumsy rage attack, not a coordinated tactical unit strike.

As she'd scrambled into the kitchen behind Owen Blake, Sogge had been raising himself from the floor, having slipped on the slanted hardboard. A clumsy, oafish entry by a confused fool.

But he had a Heckler & Koch P30 semi-automatic pointed right at them.

She raised her gun and pointed it at him before he could shoot, edging to the side so she could switch to point at

Owen Blake if she needed to. Despite his promises, he'd killed everyone.

The air crackled with tension, each of them poised to shoot.

"Drop your weapons!" Sogge yelled, his voice laced with desperation. "I'm not the enemy!"

"It looks like you are!" Larsen spat back, her eyes never leaving Sogge's.

"Kari, listen to me," Sogge pleaded. "The gang kidnapped me and Martin earlier today. I've been trying to find him ever since."

Her grip tightened on the gun, her thoughts racing. Could Sogge be telling the truth? This was what Erik had thought, and even Martin too. But this man had kidnapped her son.

"Martin's safe," she said. "He's safe where no one can find him."

Sogge heaved a sigh of relief and dropped his gun, just a fraction.

"Owen, stand down," she ordered, her voice wavering.

"Are you sure?" Owen Blake growled, his gaze and his gun still locked on Sogge. "You trust him?"

"I've been risking my life to find Martin!" Sogge shot back, frustration seeping into his tone. "Do you really think I'd be here if I didn't care about saving him?"

"Enough!" Larsen barked. She took a deep breath, trying to quell the desire to scream rising within her. "Sogge, if you're telling the truth, you'll drop your weapon."

Sogge let out a little sob. He was a sweaty mess who just wasn't cut out for this kind of activity, despite holding down a job as a cop.

Her phone rang, its shrill tone piercing through the heavy silence.

No one moved.

With her free hand, she picked it from her hip pocket and glanced at the screen.

Henrik Haaken.

Her fingers tightened around the device, and she hesitated for a moment before answering, putting him on speakerphone so they all could hear.

"Kari," Haaken's voice boomed, authoritative and commanding. "Where the hell are you? You were supposed to join me in arresting Sogge."

Larsen's eyes flicked from Owen Blake to Sogge, her mind racing. "Where is he?" she asked, her voice steady despite the turmoil inside her.

"Across town," Haaken replied, a smug satisfaction in his tone. "We've got him holed up. Get over here now. I want you to witness his takedown so we can end this once and for all."

Sogge's gaze met hers, his expression unreadable, but she could sense his anger simmering beneath the surface.

Owen Blake shifted his weight, his jaw clenched tight, his eyes narrowed, his gun still aimed at Sogge's chest.

"Are you sure it's him?" she pressed.

"Positive," Haaken responded without hesitation. "I'm looking at him right now. We don't have much time."

"And he's at the Karakkevik bar?"

"I've told you," Haaken barked. "Get here now."

"On my way," she said and hung up.

"What was that?" Sogge asked.

"Chief Haaken," Larsen replied, "he's about to make an arrest."

"Thank God," Sogge said.

"It's you, Sogge, he's going to arrest you."

48

Blackwood looked from Larsen to Sogge and back again, trying to read their expressions. He didn't understand Norwegian but he sensed that this call had changed everything.

"Everyone, lower your weapons," Larsen ordered.

With a begrudging grunt, Sogge complied.

Blackwood waited till the gun was in Sogge's pocket before he too lowered his weapon.

"That was my boss, Haaken," Larsen said, "confirming that he is a lying asshole who wants me dead and that Sogge is innocent."

"You sure?" Blackwood said.

"He just said he's looking at Sogge right this moment on the other side of the city. Where he wants me to go to witness an armed bust."

"So, it's a trap," Blackwood said. "Do you know about this?"

"Of course I don't!" Sogge spat back. "Don't you see? Haaken is the one who's behind the corruption in the police force. He's collaborating with Rune Prestegård. I even believe he was the one who murdered your husband."

"You have any proof of that?" Larsen asked.

Sogge shook his head. "But think about it. You know it makes sense."

Larsen thought about it and didn't like the thought. "All right then," she said, her tone hard as steel. "We work together. But if I find out you're lying, Sogge... there'll be hell to pay."

"You trust *him?*" Sogge sneered.

"I have to. He brought my son back to me."

Sogge's face turned stoic. He nodded and wiped his nose on his sleeve. He looked like he wanted to cry.

"Has your son ever seen Haaken?" Blackwood asked.

Larsen frowned, trying to remember. "I don't know. I don't think so."

"Then it could have been him who tried to shoot Martin this morning."

"Yes, it could."

"Can you send a photo of Haaken to Martin and get him to identify him?"

Kari nodded and picked out her phone. She rapidly scrolled the internet for a profile picture of her boss. With a few clicks, her thumbs moving at speed, she sent the photo to her son. "We should get out of here before Haaken realizes where we are."

Blackwood shook his head. "No. We have to stay here with the paintings. They're our proof."

"The paintings?" Sogge said.

"The three Munchs," Larsen said. "They're here, hanging on his walls."

Sogge gave a low whistle. "But we can't call the police, because they're not going to let us out of here alive."

Blackwood thought hard. Staying put was a death wish. They would come — what remained of Prestegård's gang, and the police too, both in cahoots — and they would take no prisoners. There was no way out of this.

"No, we can't," Blackwood said. "But we can do something else. Come with me."

49

LARSEN'S HEART RACED AS Owen Blake surveyed the room, his military instincts taking over.

"We need to prepare for a siege," he announced, his voice steady with authority. "Let's board up the kitchen."

"Right," Sogge nodded, sweat dripping down his forehead.

The three of them scrambled around the kitchen, searching for anything that could serve as makeshift tools. They grabbed frying pans, ladles, even a meat tenderizer, repurposing each one to hammer nails back into the hardboard that covered the entire kitchen window. The sound of metal clanging against metal drowned out their laboured breathing.

She hammered with a growing fury as if every nail was Haaken's face. As much as she wanted to deny it, the pieces had fallen into place before her eyes. The unexplained delays in their investigations, the lack of support from the higher-ups. It all led back to Haaken, and maybe even Kjell Thorstad above him.

"Go easy," Owen Blake said, his eyes darting to Larsen for a moment.

She paused, stifling a sob that lodged in her throat. She wanted to spit it out. Spit it right in the faces of Haaken, Kjell Thorstad, those two Internal Affairs creeps, everyone. All of them covering up her husband's murder, framing Erik to get him out of the way, murdering Jakob Varg, and Dag Engelson, the boys in the park, trying to murder her son.

She dropped the meat tenderiser. It was hopeless.

"Good work," Owen Blake said. He patted her on the back and Sogge too.

"Thanks," she replied.

"Help me with this," Owen called to Sogge, motioning toward the refrigerator, a giant silver Northland model that was almost the size of her kitchen. Together, they pulled it away from the wall, grunting with effort as they pushed it across the kitchen floor. Larsen watched, her muscles tensed, ready to act if needed.

"Almost there," Owen encouraged, his breath heavy.

Sogge's face grew red with exertion, but he didn't falter. Finally, they shoved the refrigerator against the hardboard, adding an extra layer of protection.

"Good," Owen said, wiping his brow. "That should hold."

"I hope so," Larsen muttered.

"But it won't hold for long. We need to get ahead of the game."

He stalked off out of the kitchen. Larsen and Sogge looked at each other for a puzzled moment, before rushing after him.

Owen Blake was in the vast living room, gazing at the paintings, a finger to his lips, like he was admiring the artworks in a gallery.

Sogge bundled in after her and let out a gasp. "But these really are the Munch paintings."

Sirens wailed in the distance.

Owen Blake glanced at Larsen, his brow furrowed. "They're coming," he murmured. "And you have to wonder how the police knew about this if no one reported it."

"Perhaps someone heard the gunfire and called them," Larsen offered, though she knew in her gut that the explanation was too simple, too convenient.

"Maybe," Blackwood conceded, "but do you really think that?"

Larsen clenched her fists, her nails digging into her palms. The thought of Haaken betraying her trust, endangering her son — it filled her with a cold, seething fury. She shook her head. "No, I don't," she admitted.

Blake said, "We have to show everyone that the stolen paintings are here in Prestegård's house. Give me your phone."

"Why?" she asked.

"You're going to reveal the stolen paintings and I'm going to film you doing it."

Larsen frowned. "Why not you?"

"Because it's better if it's you, the detective heading this investigation."

He was right. She could announce it to the nation, to the world, and that meant more than some foreigner, a suspected spy or terrorist with a fake name. She handed him her phone and thumbed up the camera, setting it to video.

"Wait," Owen said. "We have to set them back to how they were first, so you can reveal them."

Larsen rushed to each picture frame and pressed the buttons that slid the cheap, bad taste pictures back into view. They whirred into place, hiding the masterpieces.

"Lights," Blake said.

Sogge ran to the light switches and turned the lights on.

"Okay, ready?" Blake asked.

She nodded and took in a deep breath, taking out her ID card and holding it in front of her. Owen Blake, his face lit up with the glow from her phone, gave her a thumbs up. He was clever. He was making sure he wasn't on the film, not even his voice.

She felt an odd mix of pride and trepidation as she began. "I am Detective Sergeant Kari Larsen, of the Stovner police division, Oslo," she declared, feeling the weight of those words. "I am in the home of Rune Prestegård in the Uranienborg district of Oslo."

She gave out the full address and paused, wondering whether to admit that she had no search warrant and had broken in.

"Tonight, I responded to the sound of gunfire from within the house. The door was open. In the house there are several dead bodies of people I believe to be in the employ of Rune Prestegård. There appears to have been a devastating gun battle."

She put away her ID card and moved to the first painting. Owen Blake followed her.

"However, upon entry to the house, I have discovered a hidden cache of stolen artworks." She pressed the button and the painting of a crying clown slid up, revealing a masterpiece. "The paintings are, in fact, those stolen in the St. Petersburg gallery heist."

She moved across the room and revealed the second painting.

"As you can see, they are unmistakably the missing Edvard Munch paintings."

As soon as the second painting revealed enough of itself, she moved to the third. Blake stayed rooted to take in a wider angle, so both pictures were visible.

"And also that the stolen artworks have been installed here by Rune Prestegård, hidden from view, in his own private art gallery of masterpieces."

That was it, she thought. That was all she could say. Show the paintings and implicate him and hope that no one would question that this was, indeed, Rune Prestegård's home.

Owen Blake lifted his eyes from the phone, raising them to her.

No, there was more to say.

"I also must say that my investigation into this case has led me to strongly suspect that Rune Prestegård's criminal activities are aided and abetted by members of the Oslo police force. I intend to guard these paintings until the police come, and I will not give up this place until I can be assured that the police who are coming to the scene are not in league with Oslo's criminal underworld."

She nodded to Owen Blake and he cut the video. That was it. There was no turning back now. She had to see this through, no matter the cost.

Owen handed her phone back. "Send it to Anders Kalland at Dagbladet," he said.

Larsen's fingers shook as she typed out a message to accompany the video, then hit send. The progress bar crawled across the screen, agonizingly slow.

Sirens wailed and came closer with the roar of vehicles, many vehicles.

She ran out to the hall and peeped around the wide-open front door. Beyond the length of garden and the wrought-iron railings, police and TV crews had congregated in the street. Reporters jostled for position, setting up cameras and microphones as uniformed officers took their places around the perimeter of Prestegård's house.

"How the hell have the media got here so fast?" she said.

Blake dashed past her across the hall to the other side of the wide-open door.

Sogge came too and wondered what he should do. She signalled to the rear of the hall that led to the kitchen.

Sogge jogged back through the living room and popped his head around the second door further down the hall. She pointed to the kitchen. He nodded and turned to face it, holding his gun aloft.

"Listen up, both of you," Larsen said, her voice firm but hushed. "We're not here to kill anyone. Those are police officers outside, just like us."

Blake's jaw clenched, but he nodded.

Sogge met Larsen's gaze, determination etched into his features.

"Suppression fire only," she continued, "if it comes to that. Until we know for sure that the video is out." She checked the video's upload progress again, almost too scared to breathe.

Only fifty percent.

They checked their weapons, moving with practised precision, ensuring they had enough ammunition, each movement deliberate and calculated.

Blackwood held up the SIG Sauer P320 he'd taken from the dead guy in the hall. "This clown's shot off thirteen rounds somehow. Only five left."

"That should be enough for suppressing fire," Larsen said.

"Got it," Blake grunted. "I don't like it, but I understand."

"Good," Larsen replied, her heart pounding in her chest. They had to hold out long enough for the world to see the corruption for what it was.

"Ready?" Sogge asked, gripping his weapon tightly.

Larsen and Blackwood exchanged glances before nodding in unison.

"Ready."

She peeped out again, at the same time as Owen. They both jerked their heads back out of sight.

A figure, an officer, inching up to the gate, tiptoeing on the ice.

"Suppressing fire," Owen said, and in a flash, he jumped out and shot three times.

Before anyone could return fire, he was back against the wall, out of sight.

Voices called outside, chaos and panic.

This was it.

They were definitely in a siege.

And then the hall was full of gunfire.

50

The first shots ripped through the house like thunder. Glass shattered and splinters of wood flew through the air as bullets tore through the hall.

Blackwood pressed back against his side of the door, confident the thick wall would protect him.

Larsen cowered on the other side, covering her eyes with her arm until the fusillade ceased. Her eyes met his and she nodded, shoving down the fear, determined to stay focused.

Someone out there was still yelling out a cease fire instruction. It was a brief return of shots, nothing but a counter punch, and now things would settle down into cautious circling. They wouldn't try to storm the house, not for a while, and when they did, they would most likely come through the rear, or from upstairs.

Blackwood stepped calmly across, exposing himself for a moment in the open door, but not long enough for anyone to shoot. There were no snipers as of yet, no tell-tale beams of laser sights, and none of the regular armed cops would be quick enough to shoot just after being told to cease fire.

He walked into the living room.

"What are you doing?" Larsen hissed.

"We've got some time," he said.

Sogge turned, leaning in the door frame further down, sweat dripping from his pasty face. "What's happening?"

Blackwood's hand shot out to grasp the TV remote from the coffee table, flicking it on with a determined press of a button. The giant flatscreen flared to life. A few channels along, he found what he was looking for.

A night scene of police vehicles far off, their lights flashing, and beyond them the illuminated house. A reporter clutched a microphone with a TV News station logo and talked in rapid Norwegian.

"What are they saying?" Blackwood asked.

Larsen slipped into the living room, hovering in the doorway, reluctant to leave her post at the front door. "They're saying it's a police siege. They don't know why. But they believe it's connected to the shootings this morning. It might be that Oslo police have cornered the killers."

The reporter stepped aside and the camera zoomed in as far as it could, showing the gate, the snowy garden and the open front door.

"Damn it," Sogge whined. "They're twisting our story."

"It's what the police will be feeding them," Blackwood said. "I guess pretty soon, they'll name us and paint us as the corrupt ones."

The live video feed of the siege disappeared and was replaced by stills of Dag Engelson, and the two boys who had been shot at Middelalderparken. Then there was brief VT from earlier today in the park, showing the bodies of the boys being stretchered away. And back to the siege.

"Now they're mentioning that it's Rune Prestegård's house," Larsen said. "This will be interesting."

There was an interchange of debate between a slick newsreader in the studio and the female reporter on the scene.

"Yes," Larsen continued. "They're saying he has nothing to do with it and his house has been stormed by a criminal gang."

The feed cut to another part of the city, which looked like the main square. Ingrid Borstad stood tall and composed at the Rådhus, microphones shoved under her nose, a slick politician making a resolute statement, her cold blue eyes glaring with quiet intent.

"Jesus. She says Rune Prestegård is a respected philanthropist, donating to the city's clean-up campaign, and for that he has been targeted by the criminal gangs plaguing our city. His house has tonight been attacked by these criminals and the police are working hard to root them out."

"Fuck this fucking nazi," Sogge spat.

Larsen rolled her eyes and let out a cry of frustration.

"What?" Blackwood asked.

"She says she has strong intelligence that there are elements within the police force who are working with the criminals. There are police officers colluding with a foreign criminal and terrorist suspect who was behind the shootings today. These corrupt police officers will be dealt with."

"Shit," Blackwood said. "I guess that's me."

"And us," Larsen said. "We're the corrupt police in league with the criminal gangs."

Sogge said, "And Rune Prestegård is the innocent one."

"Any update on that video file?" Blackwood asked.

Larsen dug in her pocket and pulled out her phone. "Damn, still twenty-five percent to go."

Blackwood thought hard. It was clearly Rune Prestegård who was running the entire operation. He'd alerted his gang to Blackwood's break-in, hoping to dispose of him quietly. When that failed, he'd called Haaken and ordered police intervention. He probably even had the TV news ready to go at his whim. Or maybe it was Ingrid Borstad who handled the media.

Whatever, the story was taking shape and it was all leading to one inescapable conclusion: a shoot-out that would leave them all dead and framed for everything.

He checked his wristwatch reflexively, even though the time was clearly there on the television.

They had ten, maybe fifteen minutes, before it was all over.

"Detective Sergeant Kari Larsen!"

They all flinched at the voice, booming, too close. A loudhailer.

Blackwood rushed back to the front door and peeked out for just a second. Larsen rushed in behind him and did the same.

An older man, standing in the gate, his face hidden by a blue megaphone. In just that single second, Blackwood could see the man was late fifties, plain clothed, wearing a suit and a raincoat, no hat, an untidy mop of dark hair. Unarmed, as far as he could tell.

"It's Haaken," said Larsen.

The voice boomed through the loudhailer again. A short burst of Norwegian.

"He says he wants to come in and talk," Larsen said. "He says he's unarmed."

"Is he serious?" Sogge muttered from down the hall.

"It's probably a trap," Blackwood growled, his fingers tightening around the grip of his gun. "He wants to get in here and survey the situation."

Larsen bit her lip, weighing the risks, her mind racing. She took a deep breath, her resolve solidifying.

"Let him in," she said.

51

Blackwood watched Haaken inch up the path, hands raised, and step into the hall. The police chief gasped at the destruction and the bodies lying there.

"That's Kjetil Bergman," Blackwood said, his gun aimed at Haaken's head.

Haaken frowned and took Blackwood in with renewed interest, sizing him up.

Blackwood waved him into the living room and stayed in the door frame, one eye on the front door.

Larsen locked eyes with Haaken, her jaw set. "Talk." Her voice dripped ice.

Haaken's shoulders slumped and he lowered his hands. "Look, I want this whole situation resolved without any more shooting. Let's end this now."

"End this?" Larsen's glare bore through him.

Sogge piped up from the rear door. "It's you who's behind it all, Haaken. You killed Kari's husband. You're the corrupt cop who's in bed with Prestegård and Borstad."

Larsen smiled bitterly. "That's Sogge, by the way. Here, with me. Not across the city where you said you were watching him."

Haaken held up his palms. "I was mistaken. Clearly. I'm just trying to get at the truth, Kari."

"Truth?" Larsen spat. "You're in bed with Prestegård. And you killed my husband in cold blood." She trembled with rage. "Admit it, you bastard."

Sweat beaded Haaken's brow. His eyes pleaded, his voice calm. "I admit nothing. But we can fix this, together. No one else needs to die today."

Sogge shook his head in disgust.

Larsen scowled, clenching her fists. "The truth about you is going to come out."

Blackwood kept watch on the open door, senses alert. This was all just a cover for an attack, he was sure of it. The television was still babbling news speculation about the siege with studio talking heads debating and an inset of video footage of Haaken entering the house.

Haaken laughed, a hollow sound. "Look at you, pointing fingers. What about Larsen and Sogge? Both implicated in corruption, and now this," he gestured around the room, his eyes narrowing, "burgling Rune Prestegård's house." His gaze shifted to Blackwood, a sly grin appearing on his face. "And don't forget your new friend here – a wanted man, a foreign agent who has tried to murder a respected philanthropist."

Sogge piped up. "We know the truth. Your web of lies ends here."

Haaken smirked. "My word against criminals and cop-killers? Good luck."

The buzzing in Blackwood's pocket made him jump. He pulled out his phone.

A message from Erik.

"The operation in Stovner this morning," Blackwood said, his voice low and controlled, "was an attack on a rival criminal gang. Kjetil Bergman's crew, which is run by Rune Prestegård, is looking to wipe out the competition. The shooting at Middelalderparken targeted another gang trying to cut in on their territory. But Martin arrived just as someone else shot those boys. That someone chased Martin and tried to kill him."

The room fell silent, save for the ragged breaths of its occupants and the babble from the television. Blackwood saw the flicker of fear in Haaken's eyes and couldn't help but feel a small sense of satisfaction.

"And now Martin is going to identify you."

Haaken paled. "I don't know what you mean."

"Martin is going to identify you and testify in court."

Haaken laughed uneasily, attempting to regain some semblance of control. "Who's going to believe a teenager involved in a drugs gang," he sneered, "who most likely shot the boys from a rival gang?"

Blackwood didn't miss a beat. "We also have proof that Rune Prestegård has the paintings and that the paintings passed through your hands. Jakob Varg's appointment diary names you."

"No, it doesn't!" Haaken barked, then held his tongue, knowing he'd said too much.

"And we also have proof that you shot Kari Larsen's husband."

"Enough!" Haaken protested, his face growing red with anger. "It wasn't me!"

"It *was* you," Larsen yelled, her voice cracking with raw emotion. "All along it was you. Plotting and scheming as you were by my side."

Haaken shook his head and glanced around nervously, cornered, like a wounded animal ready to lash out. He glanced over Blackwood's shoulder and licked his lips.

Blackwood glanced out to the hall, checking on the front door. Dark figures crept along the perimeter of the grounds. Haaken's attempt to parley was all a distraction. A ruse to cover an imminent attack.

A gunshot exploded in the room.

Blackwood whipped back to see Haaken and Larsen locked in struggle, fighting over a handgun. Haaken had been armed after all. He should have frisked him.

Larsen wrenched Haaken's arm down.

The gun went off.

A loud bang echoed through the room, followed by Haaken's howl of pain. He crumpled to the floor, clutching his bleeding leg.

Blackwood couldn't help glancing at the television.

A startled reporter. Sudden panic at shots from inside the siege house. Dark figures were darting along the house front towards the open door.

In an instant, he turned and fired off three rounds out into the snow, and kicked the door shut.

Back on the television, the troops had paused, frozen against the front of the house.

Blackwood reached down and snatched up Haaken's pistol, a Heckler & Koch P30. His fingers moved deftly over the gun, checking the clip and ammunition, muscle memory from years of military training.

Another sixteen rounds.

He dropped the Sig Sauer to the floor.

"I said no killing," Larsen barked.

"No one's been killed," Blackwood responded. "But they're coming in and we have to hold them back."

52

As if on cue, glass shattered somewhere upstairs and the sound of boots pounding on wooden floors followed.

"Give up," Haaken sneered. "It's over."

Blackwood yanked him up by his collar and dragged him to the open door to the hall. In a stranglehold, he shoved the police chief ahead of him, using him as a shield and fired off three shots at the upper floor.

Troops who had been cautiously peering out jerked back out of sight.

Three neat holes in the wall above the balustrade.

Haaken shouted. *"Ikke skyt! Jeg blir holdt som gissel!"*

At the top of the marble staircase, peeking out on one side the muzzle of a Heckler & Koch MP5. On the opposite side, a small mirror.

Using Haaken's shoulder to steady his hand, Blackwood shot out the mirror.

"Ikke skyt!" Haaken yelled, weeping.

Down the hall, Sogge appeared at the rear door to the living room, sheltered under the balcony. He turned and aimed at the front door. That made sense. Someone still needed to cover the rear entry point from the kitchen, and Blackwood's current position made sense to do that. They could shoot past each other without danger.

But that left no one to cover the attack from the balcony.

"Larsen! Cover me!" he yelled.

She came to his side, her weapon drawn, and aimed it at the balcony.

"Now!" he cried.

Larsen fired off a couple of shots, sending a burst of rounds upward. The wooden balustrade splintered.

Blackwood shoved Haaken out across the hallway. The old man cried out in terror, *"Ikke skyt! Ikke skyt!"*

He landed hard against the opposite wall, behind the open front door. Dangerously exposed to the troops up on the balcony, but with Haaken as his shield.

"Larsen, you cover the rear door. The kitchen."

"Yes!" she called and retrained her sights.

"Sogge, stay on the front door!"

"Copy that!" he shouted.

The stench of gunpowder filled the air. Blackwood's gaze fell on Kjetil Bergman, lying in the middle of the hallway, his lifeless eyes staring up at the skylight. Would they come in that way, through the roof? Perhaps, but if they knew their targets were in the hallway and armed, they might not risk it.

Sogge fired off a few rounds that fizzed past Blackwood. Part of the door frame exploding in a shower of splinters. Whoever was out front, retreated fast.

Then came a great boom from the rear of the house.

The hardboard that covered the entire kitchen aperture was being pounded open.

"They're coming through the kitchen!" Larsen yelled.

"Suppressing fire!" Blackwood retorted.

She fired off a couple of shots. Something metallic zinged and chimed.

The pounding did not stop. There was a great creak as the hardboard tore free and fell. And then the giant fridge toppled with a boom.

Larsen fired off a few steady shots, which sounded like they were hitting Rune Prestegård's expensive fridge.

Up on the balcony, troops came out of cover and shot, and the hall was a typhoon of gunfire.

It was futile — they were outgunned, outnumbered, and trapped.

A scream tore through the chaos, a sharp knife cutting the air.

Blackwood's gaze snapped to Larsen, her face contorted in pain. Blood seeped between her fingers. She crumpled and fell back into the living room.

53

A SUDDEN CLATTER ECHOED through the hall, followed by the hiss of a smoke grenade.

Thrown through the front door.

Sogge shot, but it was too late.

The cannister skittered across the marble and hit Kjetil Bergman's corpse.

Blackwood shoved Haaken around to face the front door while shooting a rapid burst of fire at the balcony behind.

Bullets tore through the marble around him, chips and dust flying like shrapnel.

Dragging the police chief back, steadily emptying his clip at the balcony, he came to Kjetil Bergman's body, dropped his gun, snatched up the smoke grenade and launched it.

It struck the railing, bounced, and skittered along the landing, spewing a thick cloud of smoke that obscured their assailants.

Coughs and shouts came from the fog up there.

"Fall back!" he ordered, shoving Haaken into the living room and slamming the door shut behind him.

Sogge did the same and for a moment the inferno of the hall was muffled, distant.

He threw Haaken to the floor beside Larsen's prone body.

"Block the doors!" Blackwood grunted, pushing an overturned couch against the door as a makeshift barricade.

Sogge, breathing heavily, shoved a heavy wooden bookcase against his door.

In a mad scramble, they added more furniture – chairs, a coffee table, anything they could find – to strengthen their defence.

"Is this enough?" Sogge asked, his eyes darting to the doors as if expecting them to burst open at any moment.

"Has to be," Blackwood replied, rushing to Larsen.

He pulled her up to a sitting position against the wall.

She choked and coughed, clutching her shoulder with a red hand, the blood staining her tattered sleeve. "Fuck! This hurts!"

"How bad?" Blackwood asked, moving to inspect her shoulder.

"Could be worse," she gritted out, her face twisted in pain. "I can still move my arm."

"Keep your hand pressed on the wound—" Blackwood began.

"I know, I know." She waved him away, sweat beading her forehead, determination etched on her face.

Haaken chuckled. "What do you think you can do?"

Blackwood swung round to him, suppressing the urge to shoot him dead right there. The police chief's face was pasty white, his left leg stained wine dark. He wouldn't last another hour, maybe a half hour, losing blood at that rate.

"Just give up," Haaken wheezed. "It's over. You've lost."

Outside, the dull thud of their boots coming down the marble stairs, and more through the kitchen and the front door. They were cautiously filling the giant hall, waiting for the smoke to clear and assessing the danger.

Soon, they would start smashing at the doors.

Sogge slumped down on the floor. Blackwood read it in his face: defeat.

"Please tell me that video was sent."

Larsen fumbled in her jacket pocket, winced in pain, her hand fell limp. She croaked, "Get my phone."

Blackwood reached across and took it from her pocket. "Yes," he confirmed. "It's gone."

"What video?" Haaken asked, a thread of panic in his voice.

"The paintings," Larsen croaked. "Proof that the stolen paintings are right here in Rune Prestegård's house."

Haaken gazed at the walls and noticed them afresh. Three stolen masterpieces. He swore under his breath and clutched his leg again, wincing in pain.

But he was right, Blackwood thought. This was all they had. Martin could point the finger and identify him as the killer, but no one would believe him. Only the paintings carried any weight. And only Kalland could do anything about it.

Haaken let out a cry of pain and anger and rolled over.

Blackwood stared, caught out.

The Kahr P9 he'd thrown earlier, lying there just out of reach.

He snatched up the Sig Sauer – it had two rounds left, didn't it? – and spun round to face a gun barrel.

Their guns were almost kissing, both aimed just shy of each other. Aimed at each other's faces. One wrong breath and they would both be dead.

Blackwood swallowed hard. "Don't be stupid," he growled, trying to keep the fear from his voice.

"I'm not going to prison," Haaken replied, cold and determined.

The seconds stretched out.

"Drop it!" Sogge cried. He had his own gun trained on Haaken.

Larsen gasped. "Please, all of you, drop your weapons. No one has to die."

"I'm not going to fucking prison," Haaken hissed.

He swallowed and blinked, readying to shoot. Blackwood read the decision right there in his eyes.

Both guns went off at once and Blackwood was blinded by the flash of light before him.

54

Both doors exploded inward, wood splintering. Larsen winced in pain as she put her hands on her head. Across the room, Sogge did the same.

The troops shoved against the barricades of furniture, heaving them slowly till each door had enough access for the armed troops to swarm inside.

"Hands where I can see them!" one of the officers barked, his machine gun aimed at Larsen's head.

She laughed and it hurt.

All the troops were shouting, sweeping the room with their guns.

The troops fanned out, boots crunching on debris.

One approached the body face down on the floor.

The officer nudged him with the toe of his foot and asked, "Is it–"

"Yes, it's Owen Blake. He's dead," Larsen said, her voice steady, belying the hammering of her heart.

The officer took off his glove and knelt, fingers pressed to the dead man's neck. He looked up and gave a sharp nod.

"Haaken's alive," she said, wanting to point to the other body, but keeping her hands firmly on her head. The pain throbbed in her shoulder.

They checked him and turned him over, his one trouser leg almost black with the blood he'd lost, his raincoat flopping open. His face was all bloody, unrecognizable. He was breathing in short, ragged gasps.

"He's going to die if you don't get him help," she croaked.

"Paramedics!" one of the officers barked, and within moments, the medical team rushed in with a gurney. They moved quickly, assessing Haaken's condition, checking for any life-threatening injuries.

As they placed an oxygen mask over his face, the paramedics carefully lifted Haaken onto the stretcher, securing him before wheeling him out of the room.

Haaken's eyes found Larsen's again before the paramedics wheeled him away. She read the message there.

Thank you.

Larsen took a deep breath as she surveyed the aftermath of the siege. Broken furniture, bullet holes in the walls, blood staining the floors. But the three paintings still intact on the walls.

The gang of armed officers training their weapons on her and Sogge stared. She met their hard gazes unflinchingly. Let them look. She had nothing to hide anymore.

Her eyes were drawn to the television screen on the wall and its frantic news footage, headlines scrolling along the bottom and cutting between several different feeds.

The footage showed her in this very room from an hour ago, unveiling the stolen paintings. Despite the chaos around her, she couldn't suppress a smile of grim satisfaction.

The whole world now knew about the stolen art collection hidden in this very building. Knew about the corruption that ran deep in Oslo's elite.

Superintendent Kjell Thorstad entered, his imposing figure capturing the room's attention. He surveyed the scene, his expression unreadable, then strode towards Larsen and knelt beside her.

"Can I put my hands down now?" she said. "It really hurts."

"Of course," he said. "You're wounded."

She let her arms flop to her side, a wave of sweet relief coursing through her.

"Enough!" Thorstad barked, his voice reverberating through the room. "Lower your weapons."

The armed police hesitated, then complied.

"Kari," Thorstad said softly, extending a hand to Larsen. "You need medical attention."

"I'm okay," she said, pushing his hands away and nodding her head to the TV screen.

Thorstad turned to see. The news now showed Ingrid Borstad and Prestegård being led away in handcuffs.

"It's all gone viral," Thorstad said. "The journalist from Dagbladet released a recording from Prestegård's laptop about his meeting with Ingrid Borstad. They're discussing their scheme to wipe out Prestegård's criminal rivals. And it's not looking good for Haaken either."

"If he lives," Sogge said.

Larsen let out a breath she hadn't realized she was holding. It was really over.

"Let's get you to a hospital," Thorstad said gently.

Larsen nodded, suddenly feeling the weight of exhaustion settling on her aching body.

She winced as she moved her shoulder, the wound throbbing, the sticky warmth of blood seeping through her shirt.

Thorstad put a steadying hand under her good arm and helped her to her feet.

"Let me walk out of here," she said. "Both of us."

Sogge came to join her.

"These two are free," Thorstad yelled.

The armed police officers shuffled out of the way.

Larsen walked to the door and cast one last look at Owen Blake's body.

They stepped around the broken furniture that had barricaded the door.

Larsen breathed deeply as they emerged into the hall. It was hard to believe that just moments earlier, this had been a war zone. Now an eerie calm prevailed.

Outside, the cold air stung Larsen's face. But it had never felt so sweet.

55

Superintendent Kjell Thorstad watched as the ambulance doors slammed shut, carrying Detective Sergeant Kari Larsen to safety. Another vehicle had already sped off with Haaken. His stern expression softened for a moment, concern etching lines across his weathered face. But now was the time to show strength and leadership.

He turned to the line of TV crews and reporters being held back by police barricades, their cameras pointed at him like an army of mechanical snipers. They were hungry for answers, for reassurance. Thorstad drew in a deep breath, steeling himself for the chaos ahead. This wasn't a prepared statement, but it didn't need to be. The whole world was watching, and they all knew what had transpired here tonight.

He straightened his tie and cleared his throat.

Striding over, Thorstad raised a hand to quiet the din. "Good evening," he began, his voice calm and steady despite the turmoil inside him. "I'm here to confirm that Rune Prestegård and politician Ingrid Borstad have been arrested tonight, thanks to the evidence released by Dagbladet. Evidence that clearly implicates them in criminal conspiracy."

Cameras flashed as he continued.

"I can confirm that the stolen artworks, our national treasures, are in fact in Rune Prestegård's living room, as evidenced by Detective Sergeant Kari Larsen in the video you have all seen released on social media tonight."

Thorstad could see doubt and confusion in the eyes of the journalists before him. They wanted more, but so did he. In the cacophony he heard questions about the mysterious foreigner connected to Larsen and Sogge, details on how deep this corruption ran, how many police officers were involved, how many dead bodies were inside the house. He held up his hand again.

"I can also say that, despite the accusations and speculation against her today, Detective Sergeant Kari Larsen is entirely innocent. She and her partner, Detective Constable Mads Sogge, are the ones who brought these criminal gangs to justice. They're responsible for ending the bloodshed across our city today."

"Wasn't there a mysterious foreign spy involved?" a reporter shouted, desperation painted on her face.

Thorstad's jaw tightened. "I cannot confirm whether this individual was a spy or a terrorist. However, I can tell you he died during the siege. That is all for now. We will provide further details soon."

He turned and walked briskly back to the house, leaving the reporters shouting after him. He acknowledged the police officers at the doorway and stepped inside.

In the vast hallway, he gazed up at the skylight and the starry sky. Rune Prestegård's mansion looked like it had taken a direct missile hit. A body lay in the centre of the hall and there were more upstairs on the upper floor. Miraculously, none of his officers had been killed in the siege.

He stepped into the living room and his gaze fell on the paintings lining Prestegård's walls, allowing himself a moment of peace to just take in their beauty, as if he were strolling through a gallery on a pleasant afternoon.

Exhaling slowly, he turned to the body lying prone on the floor. Owen Blake, the mysterious foreigner who had been in the heart of the storm. A white male in a bomber jacket and jeans, the soles of his heavy boots stained with blood. The black laces undone. The back of his head was a gaping red mess of an exit wound.

A paramedic turned the body over. The bullet wound was a neat round circle between the cold, lifeless eyes.

Haaken.

Thorstad's heart dropped like a stone, his stomach twisting into knots.

This was Henrik Haaken's face.

But Haaken was in an ambulance heading for the hospital right now.

"Jesus Christ," he muttered, his eyes darting around the room. How could this have happened? He clenched his fists, fury bubbling up inside him.

56

IN THE SPEEDING AMBULANCE, Blackwood lay on the gurney, playing dead. The flickering overhead light cast eerie shadows across Haaken's bloody clothes that clung to his body.

Slowly he raised his head, glancing around.

The paramedic was sitting just a foot away, eyes glued to his phone as he watched a news video about the standoff. The sirens wailed outside, drowning out any sounds he might make.

Seeing his chance, Blackwood silently pulled off the oxygen mask they'd placed over his face. Then in one swift movement, he grabbed the paramedic from behind in a chokehold. The man let out a strangled yelp of surprise and dropped his phone to the floor.

The man struggled, his legs kicking. But it took only ten seconds of pressure on his carotid artery for him to collapse and fall limp.

Blackwood released his hold and eased the paramedic's limp body onto the gurney.

"Sorry, mate," he said.

He had five minutes maximum before the paramedic awoke. Working quickly, he reached for a red and yellow jacket emblazoned with a medical cross and pulled it on over his own bloody clothing.

Just then the siren cut and the ambulance began to slow. They must be arriving at the hospital. This was his chance.

Blackwood steadied himself as the vehicle rolled to a stop. He had to get out now, before the driver opened the rear doors.

With his heart pounding, he grabbed the door handle.

He landed on his feet, glancing around swiftly to get his bearings. He was at the hospital entrance, the ambulance having joined a long queue of other emergency vehicles all lined up.

His mind raced, running through potential escape routes. The hospital loomed large in front of him, lights ablaze. Orderlies and nurses streamed in and out of the entrance.

He considered trying to slip inside, blend in and find a back way out. But no — too risky. Security would be tight.

Keeping his head down, Blackwood hurried alongside the ambulance, using it as cover. He just needed to get to the street.

From inside the ambulance, he heard a shout. The driver had discovered the unconscious paramedic. Time was up.

Breaking into a run, Blackwood sprinted into the night. He didn't look back, focused only on escape. By the time the driver came around to check, Blackwood had disappeared into the darkness.

57

Rain lashed down on Grønland, a back street overshadowed by a concrete flyover. Rush hour pedestrians hurried to and fro through snow and slush. Blackwood shivered against the biting wind, pulling his collar higher as he passed a newspaper stand.

The front pages leaped out at him. He couldn't read the articles, but the pictures told him everything he needed to know. The story of the siege, the arrests of Rune Prestegård and Ingrid Borstad, the paintings, the shootings, the corruption. The story would dominate the press for a week, at least, and somewhere along the line there would be grainy pictures of him and speculation on the mysterious foreigner.

If the police chief wanted it.

But maybe he didn't. Maybe it was best for everyone if Owen Blake just disappeared and no one talked of him ever again.

He picked up a copy of Dagbladet and dropped some coins in the vendor's palm.

Twenty feet away was a tiny boutique post office. He entered and found a shelf where he opened the newspaper and skimmed through it. He ripped out two photos — one of Haaken and another of Kjetil Bergman.

At the counter he asked to buy an envelope. The cashier spoke perfect English. He shoved the cuttings into the envelope and quickly scribbled the address he had on his phone from yesterday morning.

Gunilla Engelson's address.

She might be puzzled at first, but he hoped she would realize: the English stranger had kept his promise; that these were the men who had murdered her husband and her son. He hoped she would realize that he had given her justice.

He paid for the stamp and envelope and left the letter with the cashier, who reached behind her and popped it into a post sack.

He walked swiftly away, just like every other pedestrian in the rush hour with somewhere to go. Turned the corner and marched down an arcade sidewalk.

Pausing at a jeweller's shop window, he pretended to gaze at the gaudy necklaces and rings on display, checking the reflection of the opposite pavement.

The Rock In bar entrance was just a doorway between a greengrocer's and a kebab house.

A figure sidled down the street and approached the bar entrance – Larsen with her arm in a sling. Alone.

She paused at the Rock In doorway and pushed inside.

Blackwood turned from the jeweller's display and scanned the windows of all the buildings opposite, then the street, up and down, searching for any signs of the usual clumsy police surveillance: street sweepers working the evening shift for no reason, men reading newspapers in the dark, anyone reflexively touching an ear. But there was no one.

It seemed all clear.

He scanned the area once more, searching for hidden eyes.

Nothing.

Good.

He stepped out of the shadows, pulling his collar up against the biting wind, crossed the street and entered.

Inside the pub, it was a black hole, only the bar shining with an array of spirits, and the light above the blue pool table. Death metal played over the speakers, but reasonably low. This place would not really wake up till much later.

Larsen had taken a seat in a dark corner, well away from the handful of people in the place. He sidled over and sat opposite her before she noticed him, placing his holdall down beside him.

Her eyes widened, relief shining in their depths. "You're alive," she whispered.

She pushed a whiskey across the table to him. He nosed it and took a sip. Linseed oil and honey.

"Surprised?"

"More relieved," she admitted. "How did you stay ahead of the police?"

"I know how they think."

She looked him up and down. "But how?"

"Once I'd skipped the ambulance, I cleaned Haaken's blood off me in a public toilet, dumped the paramedic jacket. Broke into my hotel room and–"

"It was under surveillance."

Blackwood gave her a look.

"Go on," she said.

"Showered, changed–"

"You showered under police surveillance?"

He paused, taking another sip of his drink. "Collected my belongings, sneaked out."

Larsen nodded. "Of course, Kjell Thorstad has no interest in catching you. It's quite convenient that Owen Blake is dead. If you were arrested, there would be some very awkward questions."

Blackwood leaned back in his chair, affecting nonchalance. "How's Martin?"

"Fine," she replied, her voice tense. "I want to thank you for saving his life."

Blackwood nodded, wishing he could say goodbye, make sure the kid was alright.

As if reading his thoughts, Larsen's expression hardened. "I don't want him around men like you. Men who kill."

Blackwood flinched, pain radiating through him. Death — that's what he was. A killer, a harbinger of destruction. But it wasn't what he wanted to be. Not anymore.

"Sorry," Larsen whispered, regret etched into her features. "That was uncalled for."

He shook his head, swallowing the lump in his throat, looked down at his hands, imagining the blood that stained them. "No, you're right. That's who I am. But I don't want to be that."

Larsen studied him for a long moment.

A distant police siren wailed, somewhere far off across the city.

"I have to go," Blackwood said.

"Where?"

He shrugged, feigning indifference. "I don't know yet." But he did know, at least part of it. In exactly ten minutes, he would walk round the block to Oslo bus terminal and get on a coach that would take him to the small town of Halden, near the border, and an appointment with another automated parcel locker facility where a new passport and driving licence would be waiting. A new identity. After that, who knew, except after Norway he wanted it to be somewhere warm.

Larsen's eyes narrowed, and she grimaced, no doubt suspecting his reluctance to share the information. The unspoken words hung in the air between them: he didn't trust her enough to confide in her.

"Does it matter?" Blackwood countered, forcing a smile. "I'll be far away from here."

Her expression softened, but her voice held a trace of bitterness. "No. It doesn't matter."

Blackwood knocked back his whiskey in one swift motion. He savoured the subtle bloom of its finish. "Time for me to go," he said, rising from his seat.

"Goodbye," she said. "And good luck."

He hesitated for a moment, then made a decision. "My real name... it's John. John Blackwood."

The surprise in her eyes gave way to understanding, and she nodded. "Goodbye, John."

And then he walked out of the pub without looking back.

Thank you

... for reading *Death in Oslo*. If you liked it, please take a minute to write a review where you bought it. Reviews really do help me sell more books, and if that happens, John Blackwood will return in

DEATH ON THE ROCK

In the scorching sun of Ibiza, John Blackwood thought he'd left behind the blood-soaked shadows of his past. Living happily and anonymously, his peace shatters when a ruthless gang threatens his idyllic sanctuary and an old contact from his Clocktower days as an off-the-books assassin catches up with him.

Turn the page for an exclusive extract.

1

THE VOLLEYBALL WHIZZED OVER the net. Blackwood lunged, kicking up a spray of sand, his muscular frame stretching to its limits as he dived. His fingertips grazed the worn leather but it spun away, landing just inside the line.

"Yes!" the cry went up from the others.

Rosario flashed a sarcastic grin. "So close, John! You almost had it."

Blackwood pushed himself up, brushing the sand from his chest. He shook his head ruefully. "Thanks, coach."

"Oh stop," Rosario laughed. "You'll get the next one. I believe in you."

Her infectious enthusiasm made the corners of his mouth turn up. The Ibizan sun lit her olive skin with a golden sheen as she bounced on her toes, ready for the next volley.

Blackwood crouched, eyes narrowed in concentration. Rosario shuffled into position beside him, her lithe form coiled and ready to spring.

With a leaping swing, Isabel smashed the ball over. It came in hard and low, a white blur against the brilliant blue sky. Blackwood jumped, swinging his arm with brutal power.

THWACK! His palm connected, sending the ball rocketing back. Luis and Carlos dove but it struck the sand between them.

"Told you I'd get the next one."

Rosario, Elena and Miguel laughed and high-fived him.

"Never doubted you for a second."

As she jogged back to her position, Rosario's dark ponytail swished across her slim shoulders.

They all turned at a volley of raucous laughter.

The boisterous yelling of a gang of English tourists. They stumbled over to them from the beach bar, lobster red, clutching plastic glasses of cheap beer, slurring cockney.

Rosario wrinkled her nose. "Ugh. It's like this every summer. The island gets overrun by these party animals."

Blackwood chuckled, his eyes never leaving the rowdy group, heading their way.

"Can't really blame them, can you? We actually live in paradise."

Blackwood subtly shifted position, placing himself between Rosario and the group. It was an instinctive move.

"Oi, mate!" one of them slurred. "Let's have a game, eh?"

Blackwood's jaw clenched, his fingers curling into fists at his sides. He knew the type all too well – all lager bluster.

Carlos served.

The ball arced over the net. Rosario back-pedalled, eyeing it as it fell from the sky.

One of the drunks lurched forward onto the court, crashing into Rosario.

She stumbled forward.

Blackwood was there, his arms wrapping around her waist to steady her. He pulled her close and spun around, his body a solid wall of protection as he glared at the tourist.

"Watch yourself, mate," he growled, his voice low and menacing.

The tourist blinked, his alcohol-addled brain struggling to process the warning. Behind him, his friends jeered and laughed, egging him on.

Blackwood's mind raced, calculating the threat level and assessing his options. He knew he could take them all out with ease. But he also knew the consequences of such an action, the unwanted attention it would bring.

The drunk backed off, arms flailing, giving it the big one. "Come on then, you wanker!"

The rest of them cackled and gave out the same, but they all backed off.

Rosario's hand on his arm brought him back to the present. "John," she murmured, her voice soft and soothing. "It's okay. I'm okay."

Blackwood took a deep breath, forcing himself to relax. He shot one last warning look at the tourists before turning his attention back to Rosario.

"You sure you're alright?" he asked, his hands skimming over her arms and shoulders as if to reassure himself of her safety.

Rosario nodded, a small smile playing at the corners of her mouth. "I'm fine, my hero."

Blackwood returned her smile. She was taking the piss again.

"Next time I'll leave you to it," he said.

"I could take them," she laughed. "I did a judo class at school."

She threw shapes with her arms. Blackwood laughed.

"You sure it wasn't a dance class?"

"Let's have a break!" Carlos called.

They all retreated to the low beach wall and collapsed.

Rosario grabbed a water bottle and took a long swig before passing it to Blackwood.

"Good work," Miguel said. "You're a killer, man."

Blackwood forced a smile. He closed his eyes and chanted in his head, *gone, gone, gone.* A mantra he once used to push through pain. Now he used it to push away the memories: the pile of bloody corpses. So many dead at his hands

With a deep breath, he brought himself back to this moment, this time, his gaze drifting to the horizon.

Rosario's voice broke through his reverie. "John? Is everything okay?"

Blackwood turned back to her, his smile not quite reaching his eyes. "Everything's perfect," he lied smoothly.

He swept his arm to take in the spectacular view. The endless expanse of blue, the sunset, painting the sky in shades of orange and pink.

Rosario's fingers traced the jagged scar on his chest, her touch feather-light. "You go deep sometimes, don't you?" Her voice was soft, understanding.

Blackwood swallowed hard, his throat tight. He couldn't bring himself to meet her gaze, afraid of what he might find there.

"I've got resting deep face," he joked. He reached for his t-shirt, suddenly feeling exposed.

Rosario caught his hand, her grip gentle but firm. "You don't have to hide from me, John. I'm here for you, no matter what."

He opened his mouth to respond, but something caught his eye.

No, not his eye. Something caught his senses. The off-key vibration that had tickled the back of his neck for the last few minutes.

He knew that sensation, and only now acknowledged it. The sense of being watched, of eyes on him.

He turned his head, his gaze drawn to the nearby beach bar, scanning the throng of revellers.

A figure ducked away and disappeared in the crowd.

Had he been watching them?

Just one guy, older, greying hair, shades, a maroon polo shirt. That was all he'd seen in the flash of second.

Not enough to recognise him.

He put on a fake smile and turned back to Rosario.

"Hey, we should go."

2

The bass thumped through Preece's chest as he surveyed the crowded beach bar. His crew of military mates and a few civilian tagalongs had claimed a prime spot at the beachside bar, pounding back shots.

"Can't believe they wouldn't let us into O Beach, bruv!" Jonesy slurred, slamming his empty glass on the driftwood counter. "We're fucking war heroes!"

"Fuck that posh shite," Marco hollered over the music. "Plenty of booze and birds right here!"

He elbowed Preece and gestured at a group of bikini-clad girls dancing nearby.

Preece allowed a corner of his mouth to twitch up in an imitation of a grin. Just blending in with the lads, playing the game like he always did. Getting stuck in some ridiculous beach bar was far from his idea of a good time.

The civilians in their crew were already three sheets to the wind, swaying and sloshing their beers. A few of his mates joined in, singing a rugby song at the top of their lungs.

Preece scanned the perimeter out of deeply ingrained habit, marking exits and blind spots. The neon wristband marking him as part of the stag party chafed against his scarred wrist.

"Got the next round, lads!" Baz announced, dropping a tray of shot glasses filled with green liquid on their claimed patch of sand. "Stag tradition — gotta shoot the snake!"

The men whooped and grabbed for the potent liquor. Preece took one and threw it back mechanically, barely feeling the burn.

"Cheers, mate!" Jonesy, his new desk-buddy from the Ministry, clapped him on the shoulder, already well on his way to sloshed. "Thank Christ we're out of the field, eh? No more getting shot at by tangos in Tikrit!"

Preece forced a chuckle. "Too right, buddy. Riding a desk is the life now." The words tasted like ashes on his tongue.

"Damn straight! Cushy gig till retirement. Just the way I like it." The man took another shot, swaying.

Preece's fingers twitched, muscle memory aching for the familiar weight of a SIG Sauer. Picturing his hands around a rifle grip instead of a bottle of expensive piss beer.

He knocked back another tasteless drink and smiled tightly. Drinking games. Bloody juvenile. But on the outside, he was just here. One of the lads. Playing pretend.

The groom was laughing raucously now as the crew tried to make him wear some hideous sombrero with a veil. Preece watched with dead eyes and a rictus grin.

Languishing behind a desk was a special kind of hell and he was already feeling it after only a month. He needed to be out there. Not rotting in some dreary office. Withering away. Letting his deadly skills degrade.

He downed another beer robotically, and his gaze drifted, seeking any distraction from the inane festivities. The pulsing beats from the bar speakers faded into a dull thrum as his hunter's eyes scanned the shore.

There. Further down the beach. A volleyball game in full swing.

His sniper's vision zeroed in on the athletic figures leaping and diving in the sand. Bronzed skin glistening with sweat. Taut muscles flexing with each spike and dig.

The girls were something else. Lithe and agile. All long legs and toned curves poured into Lycra. Giggling and cheering as they played.

Definitely local talent. They moved with an effortless sensuality that marked them as true Spanish beauties, sand flicking off their shapely calves as they jumped for the ball.

Preece tracked their movements with a predator's focus. Ibiza certainly had its perks.

A tall brunette leaped for a spike, ponytail whipping behind her. Her skimpy red top struggled to contain her assets as she slammed the ball over the net. Preece's eyes narrowed appreciatively.

A commotion suddenly drew his gaze. A gang of sloppy drunks from their beach bar were stumbling over to the volleyball pitch. Sloshing drinks and hooting obnoxiously.

Preece sneered in disgust. Pathetic wankers. Too pissed to see they didn't stand a chance. Foolishly thinking their boorish antics would get them anywhere with those goddesses.

The brunette dove to make a dig, but a drunk blundered into her path. She collided with him and stumbled forward. One of the men caught her, glaring daggers at the drunks.

A tense standoff. The locals squared off against the pisshead tourists.

The interlopers fucked off, staggering back towards the bar, still guffawing and catcalling over their shoulders.

They jostled past Preece's table, a bleary-eyed wanker knocking into his arm. Rum sloshed over the rim of his glass, splashing sticky rivulets down his forearm.

"Oy, watch it, twat," the tosser slurred. Then he was weaving away, oblivious.

Preece set his glass down. Alcohol dripped from his clenched fist. His pulse thudded in his ears.

In a flash, he was among them. A blur of precise, ruthless strikes.

His palm smashed the nearest one's nose with a sickening crunch. Blood sprayed as the man reeled back, shrieking.

Preece pivoted, elbow cracking into another's temple. The drunk crumpled, eyes rolling back.

The third swung a wild haymaker. Preece caught his wrist, wrenching viciously. Bones snapped. The man howled.

Preece drove a knee into his groin, doubling him over. A hammer fist to the nape sent him face-first into the sand.

It was over in seconds. Three bodies lay unmoving at Preece's feet.

Chest heaving, he surveyed his work, savage satisfaction thrumming through his veins.

Preece blinked.

The men still stood by the bar. Laughing, shoving each other, spilling drinks. Untouched. The bass thud of music. Carefree chatter and clinking bottles. Salt and suntan lotion on the balmy breeze.

Preece looked down at his hand, half-expecting to see split, bruised knuckles. But the skin was smooth. Unblemished.

He shook his head, dispelling the violent fantasy. His gaze drifted back to the volleyball game, seeking distraction.

But the players were dispersing, grabbing towels and water bottles. The game was over.

His eyes snagged on a couple sitting together on the wall. The brunette, lithe and sun-kissed, was laughing at something the man said.

Preece focused on the man. Tall, broad-shouldered. Clearly fit, despite the salt-and-pepper beard. He wore his years well.

Something about him niggled at Preece's brain. A feeling of recognition, dancing just out of reach.

The man turned slightly, and Preece caught his profile. Strong jaw, Roman nose. Steel blue eyes, crinkled at the corners.

Preece froze, his drink halfway to his lips. No. It couldn't be. Not here, not now.

The man was dead.

He narrowed his eyes, studying the stranger's face. The beard was new, but there was no mistaking those chiselled features.

Realization slammed into Preece like a freight train.

It was John Blackwood.

In the flesh.

Four years ago, Blackwood had been declared snuffed, slotted, neutralised in Oslo. Preece had read the report himself.

He slipped away from the boisterous party, drink forgotten. He wove through the throngs of sunburnt, scantily clad tourists until he found a secluded spot behind a beach shack.

Pulling out his phone, he dialled a number from memory.

The line clicked and a voice answered.

"Clocktower."

Acknowledgements

I would like to extend my heartfelt gratitude to the residents of Oslo and the local cultural guides who shared their insights and stories with me. Your knowledge and hospitality were invaluable in bringing the city to life in these pages.

I am grateful to my beta readers and early reviewers for their constructive feedback and suggestions. Your keen eyes and honest opinions were instrumental in refining the manuscript.

Profuse thanks to author Jack Turner, who always provides invaluable advice on all aspects of the military, weaponry and murder.

Thanks also to everyone at Wallbank Books for their hardworking support and encouragement, but mostly to editor David Wake, who once again was unstinting in his demands for perfection. His own brilliant books can be found at davidwake.com.

And finally, to my wife, Lorna, and my friends and family, whose unwavering support and encouragement mean the world to me. Thank you for believing in me and my work, and for your patience during the long hours of writing and research.

UNLOCK THE CANTERBURY FILE

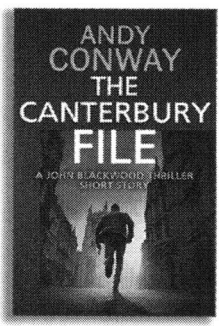

A FREE SHORT STORY PREQUEL TO THE JOHN BLACKWOOD THRILLER SERIES

Join the John Blackwood Shadow Network today and immediately receive The Canterbury File, an exclusive short story prequel only available to Shadow Network members.

Uncover the details of Blackwood's last mission for Clocktower, the off-the-books assassination squad that shaped him, and witness the betrayal that sets the stage for the entire John Blackwood Thriller series.

https://subscribepage.io/CanterburyFile

About the Author

Andy Conway is a novelist and screenwriter who publishes the John Blackwood thrillers, the best-selling Touchstone historical fantasy saga, and the Dartmoor Noir series. He lives in Birmingham with his wife and two ginger cats, and runs a publishing empire from his loft.

Also from Wallbank Books

Step into the gritty world of Howie Earls, the Black journalist who digs up the dirt other hacks won't touch.

Chuck Loyola's hardboiled crime series delivers classic private eye pulp noir with a modern edge. Think Raymond Chandler with a British accent and a protagonist who's got more to lose than just his press pass.
Available in Kindle, paperback and Kindle Unlimited.

Printed in Dunstable, United Kingdom